Jordan wanted to see Northcote Hall!

Like the rest of the villagers, Madeleine was concerned about who had bought the gracious old house. As an antique dealer, she planned to go there prior to the auction, so she agreed to drive him.

"Where would you like to start?" she asked when they arrived. "Inside or out? I could—" she broke off as Jordan raised his hand.

"You don't have to dance attendance on me, Miss Crawford," he said. "I'm sure you have plenty you want to look at. Why don't we go our separate ways and meet up again later?"

He'd done it again, Madeleine thought. His tone had been perfectly polite, his suggestion reasonable, but all the same he had managed to inject a hint of dismissal, almost a rejection into the words.

Kate Walker chose the Brontë sisters, the development of their writing from childhood to maturity, as the topic for her master's thesis. It is little wonder, then, that she should go on to write romance fiction. She lives in the United Kingdom with her husband and son, and when she isn't writing, she tries to keep up with her hobbies of embroidery, knitting, antiques and, of course, reading.

Books by Kate Walker

HARLEQUIN ROMANCE
2783—GAME OF HAZARD
2826—ROUGH DIAMOND
2910—CAPTIVE LOVER

HARLEQUIN PRESENTS
1053—BROKEN SILENCE

Man
of Shadows
Kate Walker

Harlequin Books

TORONTO • NEW YORK • LONDON
AMSTERDAM • PARIS • SYDNEY • HAMBURG
STOCKHOLM • ATHENS • TOKYO • MILAN

Original hardcover edition published in 1987
by Mills & Boon Limited

ISBN 0-373-02920-9

Harlequin Romance first edition July 1988

CHAPTER ONE

THE village hall was crowded, the subdued hum of conversation sounding in Madeleine's ears as she lifted a necklace from a display case to show it to an interested customer.

'It's Victorian jet,' she explained. 'Jet was often used for mourning jewellery, especially when Prince Albert died. But later it became fashionable in its own right. There's a bracelet to match it, too.'

'It is lovely.' The woman considered the gleaming black beads in her hand thoughtfully. 'But, really, I was looking for something a bit longer.'

'In the jet?' Madeleine took another strand of beads from the case. 'What about this? Or there's a pendant set with jet and pearls.'

She waited patiently as the customer debated her choice, finally settling on the necklace she had originally asked to see. Madeleine wrapped it in tissue paper, slipped it into a protective envelope, took the money and offered smiling thanks, then watched the woman move away into the crowd.

Another sale, she thought with some satisfaction, turning to replace the unwanted jewellery in the display cabinet. Business was quite brisk this morning. Closing the cabinet, she paused to adjust the position of a collection of old linen and lace, a faint smile curving her lips at the memory of the hard work that had gone into restoring the tablecloths, mats and runners, transforming them from the creased and yellowed condition in which she had found them in the auction room to their present sparkling whiteness. It had taken a week of evenings spent bleaching, washing, ironing and starching, but it had been worth it; already they had attracted plenty of attention from local collectors who had come to look for bargains.

'I see the weather hasn't kept the hordes away.' The ruffled, salt-and-pepper head of Elsie Peterson, who had the stall next to hers, appeared at Madeleine's shoulder. 'I might have known that a little rain couldn't stop the horsy set—they can sniff out a bargain at a distance of ten miles.'

'Hardly a little rain!' Madeleine directed a wry glance at the storm-lashed windows of the church hall, her blue eyes rueful. 'It's more like a hurricane out there.'

'Isn't it just!' Elsie shivered dramatically. 'Look, I'm dying for a coffee. Be a love, and watch my stall for a moment while I grab some refreshment. I'll get you one too—black, no sugar, that's right, isn't it?' She wrinkled her nose in distaste as Madeleine nodded. 'I don't know how you can bear to drink it that way. I won't be a sec.'

As Elsie began to push her way through the crowd, Madeleine automatically threw a glance at the adjacent table where a display of picture cards, stamps and old photographs were set out. An elderly man was sorting purposefully through a box of cigarette cards.

'Can I help you?' she asked politely, but received a shake of the head in reply.

'I'm just looking, if that's all right.'

'Of course—let me know if you want anything.'

Her own stall was temporarily deserted and she re-treated back into her own private thoughts, grateful for a few moments' peace and quiet after the bustle of the last hour to reflect on the fact that she was here at all, and to wonder at the impulse that had led her to abandon her half-formed plans for her day off in favour of this particular antiques fair.

Madeleine tossed the long plait that held her dark brown hair confined back over her shoulder, frowning slightly as she did so. Antiques fairs were one of the most rewarding aspects of her job, second only to the excitement of hunting out and bidding for bargains at auctions. Sales were important, of course, but the real interest lay in having the time to talk to the people who stopped at her stall, answering questions, advising on the date of a particular piece or its place of manufacture, and often adding a few snippets of social history along the way. That way she used the knowledge she had acquired in studying for her degree in history, as well as the business and sales experience she had picked up since.

But it was more than simple enjoyment of such occasions that had led her to come to this fair in her mother's place. She had woken this morning with a feeling of—she could only call it anticipation, a sense that something very special was going to happen. It was like the feeling she had had as child when waking on Christmas morning or her birthday, an awareness of something very important, so that, in spite of the fact that she had been out with friends the evening before, sitting talking over coffee until very late, she felt full of energy, ready for more than just a quiet day at home, and had offered to take her mother's place this morning.

But what could be

Elsie had returned, two plastic cups of coffee balanced precariously on a paper plate, which also bore a couple of rather sickly looking buns.

'Coffee's served. Have a bun.'

'Not for me, thanks.' Madeleine shook her head, sending the long dark plait flying over one shoulder. With an impatient gesture she pushed it away.

'Hey, Maddy, are you OK?' The joking tone had faded from Elsie's voice. 'You look a bit pale.'

'It's just the end-of-winter syndrome. I never have much colour at the best of times, and this weather doesn't help. We could all do with a bit of sun after the hard winter we've had.'

Perhaps she did look a little wan, Madeleine thought, catching a glimpse of herself in the glass of a framed watercolour propped up at the back of the stall. Absently she rubbed at her cheeks to bring some colour into them, considering her own face objectively as she did so.

For all her hair was so very dark, she had none of the tawny complexion usually associated with such colouring. Her skin was delicately fair—too fair, Madeleine privately believed—its colour, so often referred to as magnolia in beauty articles, more often appearing as just plain white, so that the glossy deep brown sheen of her hair appeared almost shockingly dramatic in contrast.

Still, at least she had that touch of drama, she re-

was emphasised by the way the thick brows were drawn slightly together, as if his habitual expression was a frown rather than a smile. Under the straight nose, the firm mouth looked as if it rarely curled into anything other than the hard line that made him look as if his lips were clamped shut against some biting comment.

Not an approachable face, Madeleine decided. The slightly aloof expression and something about his air and bearing gave an impression of isolation and withdrawal, for all he was in the centre of a noisy, laughing crowd. In spite of his thinness, he was broad at his shoulders and chest under a heavy Aran sweater, and he held himself well with a sort of easy, well knit power that spoke of trained muscles and, before illness had taken its toll, a perfect physical fitness. Crisp hair of the shade that would bleach gold-blond in the sun, but was now the rich colour of liquid honey, was cut close against his well shaped head, the no-nonsense severity of its style clearly meant to impose some order on a rebellious tendency to wave if it grew an inch or so longer.

'I wonder who he is.' The words escaped involuntarily, and Madeleine jumped as a hard elbow made contact with her ribs.

'Customer!' Elsie hissed and, dragging her eyes away from the sight that had held her transfixed for who knew how long, Madeleine blinked dazedly at the man whose expectant face showed clearly that he wanted an answer to some question she hadn't heard him ask.

'I'm sorry—I was miles away. What was it you wanted?'

It was perhaps half an hour later that the Evensleighs and their friends, having made the rounds of the other stalls, finally arrived in front of Madeleine's. It had been a busy half-hour for her, the man who had bought the watercolour being the first in a flurry of customers, and the bustle of activity had provided a distraction, diverting her mind into more practical channels and pushing all thoughts of the stranger to the back of her mind.

She found it difficult to suppress a prickle of irritation as she watched Rupert and his girlfriend Geraldine rooting through the collection of items on one side of the stall. She had selected everything personally, hunting through auction rooms and house sales to find things that appealed to her own sense of beauty, as well as those she knew would sell. Antiques weren't just a living to her, they were an art, and she was happiest knowing that she had sold an item to someone who would appreciate it as much as she did. So it was always a struggle to sell to people like the Evensleighs, who regarded such beauty simply as an investment, buying what was reasonable now with a view to watching it appreciate in value in a very short time. Bad for business or not, there was always a temptation to be distinctly off-putting and unhelpful to such customers, in a way that had her mother tearing her hair in despair.

So it was with very mixed feelings that she saw Geraldine sorting through the bundle of linens and embroideries, pushing aside discarded items in a way that would leave them crumpled and creased.

'Jordy's in one hell of a mood.' Rupert's voice was low and cautious as he spoke to his girlfriend, as if he wanted to avoid being overheard by some other member of their party. 'Surely he can't still be brooding over Swallow.'

'Perhaps he's missing Sukey.' There was a streak of maliciousness in Geraldine's voice, one that grated on Madeleine's nerves every bit as much as the mess

Geraldine was making of the beautiful materials. She moved forward hastily.

'Can I help you, Miss Fry?' she asked, trying to keep the sharp note out of her voice. 'Were you looking for anything in particular?'

'Oh, I'm just browsing.'

Geraldine flicked over a particularly lovely embroidered silk picture with a carelessness that had Madeleine clamping her jaw shut on an angry protest. Such pictures, framed or unframed, were hard to find, and she could vividly recall her own excitement when she had discovered this one.

'But, really, you haven't anything I like.'

'There's a lovely damask tablecloth——'

'Not for me, thanks.' Geraldine's plummy tones and her smile were tinged with condescension. 'I'd rather have that sort of thing brand new.'

Suit yourself! Madeleine was tempted to retort, but luckily, at that moment, her attention was claimed by Peter Evensleigh who strolled up to lounge indolently against one side of the table.

'Hello, Maddy. How's business? Sold much?'

'Quite a bit.' Madeleine gratefully latched on to Peter's attention, glad to be distracted from Geraldine's bargain-hunting. 'There's a good crowd here; the weather hasn't kept people away.'

Peter's aristocratic face twisted into a grimace of distaste. 'Foul, isn't it? It's raining cats and dogs out there.'

He paused and, from long experience, Madeleine resignedly prepared a smile for what would come next.

'And there's one thing worse than it raining cats and dogs—and that's when it's hailing taxis.'

On Madeleine's left, Rupert's chortle of laughter showed the appreciation she was incapable of feeling.

Peter had an endless fund of these childish jokes, dragging them into the conversation on the slightest justification, and often without any at all.

'Have you made up your mind about the Ball yet?' Peter was saying now, and Madeleine's hands curled against her sides in impotent frustration.

Couldn't Peter take no for an answer? She had made up her mind weeks ago, and had told him so three times at least, but he still persisted in ignoring her refusal, incapable of believing that she might not want to go out with him.

'I'm——' she began, but at that moment Peter moved from his perch on the table, knocking against something that fell to the floor with a clatter.

'Peter, you clumsy oaf!' Geraldine exclaimed angrily as one of the fallen walking-sticks knocked against her leg.

'Sorry, Gerry.' Peter's apology was indifferent. He bent to retrieve the sticks, straightening up again with them in his hand. 'Well now, this is interesting,' he continued, his attention caught by one particular stick made in ebony with an elongated silver horse's head forming its handle. 'Jordan!' He raised his voice suddenly. 'Hey, Jordy, look at this.'

Madeleine barely had time to register that Peter had used the same name as the one his brother and Geraldine had used before, turning her head automatically in the direction in which he was looking. She felt her heart seem to flip over as her eyes rested on the stranger who had caught her attention earlier. Silently and irrationally, she cursed Peter for distracting her so that she hadn't noticed him approach the stall in the middle of the Evensleigh group. Illogically, she felt she should have known he was there. Unlike Rupert and the others who had concentrated in a knot around the silver in the centre of the stall, he had turned his attention to a collection of old books ranged on a shelf and now he turned slowly, one leather-bound volume still in his hand.

As before, it was his stillness that Madeleine noticed, the economy of movement emphasised by the way he did not speak, but simply directed a politely enquiring glance at Peter.

'Isn't this splendid?' Peter brandished the walking-stick high in the air, narrowly missing Madeleine's ear.

The stranger's eyes went to the long cane, his expression not altering in the slightest, but Madeleine was stunned to catch the flash of anger in his eyes, so brief it was gone in a second; but in that second he had revealed a fury so savage it made her head reel. She could see no possible reason for it, though one thing was clear: whatever else this Jordan was, he was not, as she had at first assumed, simply someone who collected old walking-sticks. But then the anger faded, replaced by a calm control that made her wonder if it had ever been there at all, or if she had been imagining things.

'Come and have a look at it, old man!' Peter urged. 'And it's time you met my girl, too.'

The proprietary gesture made towards herself sent a spark of irritation flaring through Madeleine, so that she almost rounded on Peter in fury before a sudden realisation pulled her up short. It was infuriating to be termed Peter's girl when she was no such thing, but the anger she felt was out of all proportion to that small prick of pique. With a small sense of shock in her heart she realised that it was not *what* Peter had said that annoyed her, but the fact that he had said it in front of this man called Jordan, a stranger, unseen before today, and that thought rocked her sense of reality.

Why should she care if a man she didn't know got the wrong impression about her relationship with Peter? It shouldn't matter what he thought of her and yet, for some unaccountable reason, it did matter very much indeed; so much so that it had distorted her own reactions.

For a moment it looked as if Jordan was not going to move, but then he gave a tiny, almost imperceptible shrug and walked the few steps from his position at the end of the table to Peter's side, standing directly opposite Madeleine. The tiny journey took perhaps ten seconds or less, but it was more than enough to explain the hostility Madeleine had seen burning in his eyes only moments before.

From the controlled, almost elegant stillness of that tautly held body followed not the easy, strolling movement she would have expected, but an awkward, uneven limp, the man's right leg dragging stiffly with each step. No wonder he had been so violently angry at the way Peter had drawn attention to his disability so publicly. Madeleine felt a strong wave of sympathy for the stranger, but a swift glance at the closed expression on the strongly etched profile now turned towards her told her instinctively that this man would reject any such emotion, particularly from someone he didn't know.

He was examining the walking stick now, turning it over in long narrow hands, showing decidedly more care in handling it than Peter had done, Madeleine noticed, privately notching up a point in his favour. There was something vaguely odd about the way he held the stick, something she couldn't quite place, and it nagged at her in a puzzling way.

'It's very fine,' he said at last, the sound of his voice making Madeleine bite her lip in a sudden, involuntary reaction. She had been so aware of him from the moment she had first seen him that it came as a shock to realise that these were the first words she had ever heard him speak.

His voice was low, almost soft, its quiet tones in pleasing contrast to the hearty *bonhomie* of the Evensleighs, or Geraldine's plum-in-the-mouth way of speaking, but it was laced with a thread of something that made a falsehood of Peter's jovial friendliness. The two men did not like each other at all, Madeleine realised with a shock.

'But perhaps a little too ornate,' Jordan continued. 'I think not——'

This last remark was divided equally between Peter and Madeleine herself, the fleeting, half-apologetic smile that accompanied it just enough not to be insulting. But Jordan's eyes made no contact with Madeleine's, the flickering, sidelong glance sliding over her face and away again before she could gain any impression of their colour.

'That's perfectly all right——'

'Well, you must meet Maddy.' Peter's words coincided with Madeleine's own polite acceptance. 'Jordan, this is Madeleine Crawford, Holtby's prettiest antiques entrepreneur.'

With a swift movement, Madeleine was able to turn the hand she had held out to receive the walking-stick back into her keeping into one proffered in greeting as Jordan swung round to face her fully.

'Miss Crawford.' That soft, pleasant voice murmured a vague acknowledgement, and then her hand was taken in a firm grip.

'Touch of steel.' Elsie's words reverberated in Madeleine's mind, but now with a new and very different connotation. The delicate care with which Jordan had held the walking-stick had been deceptive; his grip was hard and powerful, speaking of a strength carefully controlled so as not to hurt.

Involuntarily, Madeleine's eyes were drawn to their linked fingers, her brain noting automatically the whipcord strength of the lean hand, the sinewy toughness of his wrists below the soft cream wool of his sweater. His palms were hard, too, hard as leather, and she shivered faintly at the feel of them, that eerie sense of awareness, of something beginning, something new and very important, searing through her like a flame. Who was this man? And why did he have this powerful but inexplicable effect on her?

CHAPTER TWO

'MADDY?'

For a second it was as if Peter's voice came from another world, so that she didn't recognise it, but then a slight movement of those strong fingers against her own brought her struggling back to reality like a swimmer fighting against the tide, colouring in confusion as she found that she still held Jordan's hand in hers as she stood there, lost in her own thoughts.

'I—I'm sorry.'

With an abrupt movement, she snatched her hand away as if she had been burned, her sense of disorientation increased by the realisation that Jordan's eyes were on her face, clearly noting the betraying change in colour that she was unable to disguise. Her awkward apology was interrupted by Peter's laughter.

'Do you usually have this effect on women, Jordan? I have to admit I've never seen Maddy so disconcerted.' There was an undertone of—what? Jealousy?—running through his words, an edge that Madeleine now realised had darkened his laughter, too.

'It's not what usually happens,' Jordan responded, and now, at last, his eyes met Madeleine's fully. Having expected something darker, she found that their light, smoky grey came as something of a shock. Just for a second she was subjected to an electrifying, appraising glance, but then the spark of interest, if that was what it had been, died and she could almost hear steel doors banging shut against her as his pale face became a mask:

remote, cold, and oddly wary. 'I'm sorry if Peter led you to expect that I would buy this,' he went on, holding the walking-stick out to her.

'That doesn't matter at all, Mr——?' To Madeleine's consternation she found that her voice still sounded distinctly shaken.

'Sumner—Jordan Sumner.' It was Peter who supplied the name, and something about his tone and his expression told Madeleine that he expected she would have heard it before, that he anticipated an excited response.

Well, if that was the case he was doomed to disappointment. The name Jordan Sumner meant nothing to her, arousing no feeling beyond a sense of relief at the fact that she now had a name to put to the man who had aroused such a heightened sensitivity in her from the moment she had first seen him. Perhaps it would have helped if she *had* recognised his name. It might have gone some way towards explaining the intensity of her reaction.

'Oh, isn't this quaint!' Her thoughts were interrupted by an exaggerated squeal of delight from Geraldine Fry. 'Rupe, darling, look at this! I just have to have it!'

'This' was an Art Deco tea service in jade green, the cups and teapot cube-shaped and the saucers and plates square. Personally, Madeleine considered it rather ugly. The nineteen twenties were her least favourite period for collecting, but she realised that Art Deco was currently enjoying a vogue and so, in spite of her own reservations, she had recently bought several items in this style, one of which was the tea set.

Rupert had now joined his girlfriend, evidently sharing her delight in the squat little cups and saucers, and Madeleine couldn't resist a swift glance at Jordan

Sumner's face, to see how he was taking their display of enthusiasm. Grey eyes met blue for a second, then flicked away again, but not before Madeleine had caught the glint of horrified amusement that mirrored her own feelings exactly.

So Art Deco was not Jordan Sumner's sort of thing, either, Madeleine reflected as she wrapped the tea service in old newspaper and placed it carefully in a cardboard box for Rupert to carry home. But then, she had already decided that Jordan wasn't a typical member of the Evensleigh 'horsy set'. That thought brought memories of the air of isolation she had sensed in him at first, making her wonder if he was a 'horsy' person at all.

He had returned to his browsing among the books now, picking them up and flicking through them with that odd use of his hands that she had noticed before. She finished packing the tea set, took the money for it, and Rupert and Geraldine, triumphant at their purchase, moved on to another stall.

'You didn't recognise Jordan, did you?' Peter was still lounging against the table.

'Should I have done?' Madeleine didn't trouble to keep the tartness out of her voice. Peter wasn't her favourite person at the best of times and, still smarting from that possessive and unwarranted 'my girl', she found that his incredulous and almost reproachful tone grated unpleasantly.

'The World Championships,' Peter prompted. 'Badminton.'

'Badminton?' Madeleine echoed blankly, thinking of rackets and shuttlecocks.

'The three-day event.' Peter's explanation came impatiently.

'Oh, *that* Badminton.'

Madeleine's eyes slid to where Jordan still stood at the far end of the table, completely oblivious to their conversation. So he *was* a horsy type after all. She should have expected that; why else would he be with Rupert and Peter? But she wasn't prepared for the pang of disappointment that shot through her at the thought that Jordan *was* just one of the Evensleigh's county friends, when she had believed he was something different.

'He rides?' she said stiffly.

'Rides!' Peter's voice was filled with an exasperated condescension. 'Really, Maddy, don't you know anything? He won Badminton four times and was in the British team for the World Championships. He's one of the very best—or he was——' He broke off abruptly as Jordan approached, several books in his hand.

'I'll take these. Will a cheque be all right?'

'Of course, that'll be fine.' Still at the mercy of her confused and disturbing reactions to him, Madeleine had to work hard to keep her tone and smile neutral.

'Books, Jordy?' Peter laughed. 'I'd have thought you'd had enough of them in hospital.'

'I found a couple of Dickenses to complete a set I have at home.'

The explanation came easily, but once more Madeleine caught the edge of suppressed anger that sharpened the quiet voice. Was it the shortening of his name that he objected to? That was something she could understand. After twenty-four years, she had become resigned to being called Maddy, but deep down she disliked the abbreviated version of her name. Very few people actually used her proper name, even those who started out calling her Madeleine usually resorted to the easier Maddy after a while. But in Jordan's case she felt it was more than that. Peter's laughter had had an ugly note to it, reminding her of his comments earlier when she hadn't realised just who the 'Jordy' they spoke of was.

'Who shall I make this out to?' Jordan had pulled his cheque book from his pocket and was waiting with it open.

'Oh—L and M Crawford.'

"L and M?' Jordan repeated. 'Your husband?'

'No—my mother.' The enquiry startled Madeleine. Somehow, she hadn't expected even such a small indication of interest from this man, and, possibly even more disconcerting, the question revealed just how little credence Jordan had given to Peter's possessive 'my girl'.

'Lucy Crawford,' Peter put in.

'Lucina,' Madeleine corrected stiffly. Like herself, her mother preferred the full version of her given name. She saw those light grey eyes flick from her indignant face to Peter's unconcerned one and back again before Jordan bent to write the cheque.

Watching the precise italic script flow over the paper, Madeleine found her attention caught and held, fascinated by the movement. So that was the explanation for the apparent awkwardness she had noticed earlier. Jordan Sumner was left-handed. Just in time she pulled her gaze away, as the cheque was torn from the book and Jordan glanced up again, holding out the slip of paper and the necessary plastic card.

Checking the number and the firm slash of a signature, Madeleine automatically noted the name of a Buckinghamshire branch of the bank on the cheque in her hand. Jordan Sumner was a long way from that home he had referred to.

'Are you here on holiday, Mr Sumner?' she asked as she returned the card.

'No, this is more of a business trip. I'm thinking of buying a house up here.'

'Jordan's interested in Northcote Hall,' Peter put in. 'He's here for the auction.'

'Really?' Madeleine's interest was mixed with apprehension. Remembering what Peter's family had done to the manor, she prayed Jordan didn't have similar plans for Northcote, one of her favourite of the local old houses. But the memory of the delicate care with which he had handled the walking-stick made her think better of her unjustified suspicions. 'I'm going to the Hall tomorrow,' she added conversationally, 'to look around in preparation for the sale of contents on Monday. It's a beautiful old house, isn't it? But rather large for one person. I always thought it needed a family there. Do you have children?'

Jordan shook his head. 'I'm not married.'

Peter was getting restless. His brother and friends had collected in the doorway and were making impatient gestures to him to hurry up.

'The others are waiting...'

His voice faded before Jordan's calmly unperturbed look, and Madeleine could not resist a slight smile at this further evidence that Jordan Sumner was his own man, one who did not jump at the Evensleighs' call.

'I'll see you in the car, then——'

Jordan's nod was dismissive; his attention had apparently drifted to a box of lead soldiers on the table in front of him. Madeleine had the strangest feeling that he was lingering deliberately, though for the life of her she could not see why.

'Well, I'll be off,' Peter said awkwardly. 'I'll call round next week, Maddy, and you can tell me your decision about the Ball.'

The man was impossible! Madeleine's breath hissed between her teeth in an expression of exasperation as Peter strolled away.

'*Not* a welcome invitation,' a quiet voice said drily and glancing, startled, in Jordan's direction, Madeleine found that he had looked up from the soldiers and was watching her, amusement lighting his eyes and making them seem almost silver in the weak sunlight that had chased the storm clouds from the sky. 'Do I take it you will not be partnering Peter at the Ball?'

'N-no.' Madeleine stumbled over the word, confused by the sudden change in his mood and the transformation that took place on his face when he smiled. The mask of careful indifference broke up and all at once he looked younger, quite approachable, and much more attractive than she had first thought. She hadn't considered his age before, but without that smile she would have put him at a year or two older than Rupert's thirty-four. Now she felt he was possibly nearer to Peter, who was four years younger than his brother.

'You don't seem to have got your message across.'

'I try,' Madeleine sighed, 'but Peter's so thick-skinned he never knows when he's not wanted.'

'No.' There was more than polite agreement in the single syllable. Jordan replaced the small red-coated figure in its box with care; he seemed to be considering exactly how to phrase his next remark, but when it came it was not at all what Madeleine had expected. 'I wonder if I could ask you a favour.'

'Me?' To her embarrassment, it came out as a startled squawk. 'What sort of favour?'

'I'd like to see Northcote Hall.'

'But—I——' Thoroughly disconcerted, Madeleine found she was stammering incoherently, her confusion increased by the calm, direct look that was levelled at her face. 'But I thought you'd been round it already.'

'Under the supervision of an overly officious estate agent, yes.' Jordan's tone left her in no doubt that he had not enjoyed the experience. 'You must know what that's like. "This is the reception hall, please note the impressive ceiling with its fine moulded cornice..." You know the spiel.'

'Oh, I do!' In spite of her confusion Madeleine found herself laughing at his close parody of a local estate agent's oily tones. 'It must be very hard to really look at a place when Mr Stewart's in full flow.'

'It is. So I'd like a second look in peace and quiet, and——'

There was the briefest of pauses, an even swifter flick of his eyes in the direction of his damaged leg.

'And as I can't drive myself yet, I need someone to transport me there and back.'

Was it only the effect of the stronger light since the sky had cleared, Madeleine wondered, or was simply standing on that injured leg tiring him? His pallor seemed more pronounced, and she was sure that the fine lines that feathered out from those smoky eyes hadn't been drawn with such severity only minutes earlier. The harsher lines scored around that firm mouth seemed to have deepened too, dragging his lips down at the corners.

Hospital, Peter had said. Perhaps he had only just been discharged. Briefly, she considered offering him a chair, but the memory of the flash of anger she had seen in his eyes when Peter had drawn attention to his disability shrivelled the words on her tongue and had her blundering into an unconsidered question instead.

'But wouldn't the Evensleighs take you?'

She knew the answer as soon as she had uttered the words, reading it in Jordan's eyes which gleamed silver-light.

'Would *you* want to browse around Northcote with dear Peter or Rupert in attendance?' he shot back.

'Not on your life!'

The dry humour in Jordan's tone brought a bubble of laughter into Madeleine's throat, so that her words came out a trifle breathlessly, all the more so because there had been such an empathy in that sly glance, a world of understanding in the words implied behind what he had actually said. It was the sort of exchange she might have had with one of her sisters, where on one level nothing was said because nothing needed to be said; after years of growing up together they had arrived at a point where sometimes words were quite unnecessary. But she found it almost shocking to discover that she felt such an empathy with a man she had known for less than an hour.

'So you can understand that I prefer to go with someone rather more——' Jordan chose the word carefully '—sympathetic. You said you'd be going to Northcote tomorrow, so I wondered if you'd mind giving me a lift there.' She was treated to another of those rare smiles. 'I really would be most grateful.'

'Of course I will.'

Hey, hold your horses! the rational part of her brain reproved her hastily. This man is a *stranger*, someone you don't know. With a carelessness that was alien to her normally cautious nature, Madeleine shrugged off the mental warning. Jordan Sumner was no casual hitch-hiker picked up at the side of the road, bringing with him the threat of violence and assault. Her innermost instincts told her she could trust him, and they had never been wrong before. Besides, with that smile had come a sudden rush of wanting to know more about him, a need that went far beyond the bounds of natural curiosity.

She felt as if something was unfurling inside her, like a plant uncurling and reaching out towards the sun. In the same way she wanted to reach out to Jordan, touch him somehow as he unknowingly had touched her. It would be easy to say that he simply intrigued her, but when the time and place of their meeting had been arranged and she watched him limp away, Madeleine had to admit to herself that it was more than that. From that moment of acute physical awareness when she had touched his hand she had been caught, gripped by a sensitivity, a heightened response, that would give her no peace until she found out the reasons for it.

'It's a beautiful day, isn't it? Such a contrast to yesterday.'

Madeleine knew she sounded nervous—even in her own ears her voice was unnaturally bright and cheerful— but the plain truth of the matter was that she *was* ill at ease. It had been one thing to agree to this trip on an impulse the day before, quite another to round the bend in the road that led to the Manor and see Jordan waiting at the end of the drive, and know that they would spend much of the day together—and that she had no idea what to say to him once the conventional greetings had been exchanged.

'The forecast is good, too,' she continued, moving back from having pushed the passenger door open. 'Clear skies and reasonable temperatures. Can you manage?'

'I'm fine.' The answer came curtly as Jordan eased himself stiffly into the seat beside her, manoeuvring his damaged leg awkwardly in the confined space.

He leaned back against the seat with a faint sigh of relief, stretching his right leg out in front of him. Against the darkness of the navy shirt and jacket he wore, his pallor seemed worryingly evident and Madeleine was glad that, remembering his injury, she had thought to push the seat back as far as it would go. Even so, leg room in a Mini was limited, and if Jordan had been as tall as Peter he would have been distinctly uncomfortable. She waited until Jordan was settled before turning the key in the ignition and swinging the small black car out into the quiet country lane.

'What did you do—to your leg, I mean?' The question slipped out as a way of making conversation before she had time to think that he might not want to talk about his disability. Her uncertainty increased as she caught the hesitation before he spoke.

'I broke my thigh.'

The stark, unembroidered reply fell into the air like drops of ice, making Madeleine shiver in spite of the warmth of an early spring sun shining through the windows.

'In a riding accident?' she asked carefully.

Again there was that tiny hesitation. Jordan's eyes were fixed on a point straight ahead, far beyond the windscreen.

'Yes,' he said tersely.

It was disturbingly easy to catch and interpret the signals he was giving out. Back off! Keep out! It was clear in every line of his tense body, his hostility reaching her as if on the air, making her intensely aware of the compact strength of the man beside her, so that the space inside the car seemed suddenly confined and claustrophobic.

'I'm sorry. You don't want to talk about it.'

'No.' The single syllable was hard and unyielding. Those steel doors had slammed shut again—right in her face this time.

Biting her lip, Madeleine slowed the car at a cross-roads as she mentally cursed herself for her mistake in bringing up the subject at all. It seemed she had driven him away from her from the start, so that there was no chance of recapturing that unexpected empathy she had sensed the day before. Or had that empathy ever been there at all? Waking this morning and looking back over the events of the previous day, she had to admit to having had doubts about her own reactions, wondering if perhaps she had over-exaggerated things foolishly.

It was as they moved on again that Jordan stirred in his seat and spoke once more.

'No, I'm the one who's sorry. You were only being polite.' He pushed his hands through his hair in a gesture of tiredness and unease. 'I don't find it easy to talk about,' he went on with obvious understatement. 'I spent weeks in hospital, what seemed like an eternity in a plaster cast—and all that time the only topic of conversation was *this*!'

The last words grated through clenched teeth as he slammed one hand against the navy cord material that covered his damaged thigh, his face burning with an impotent fury that tore through Madeleine's heart like a red-hot arrow.

'That's the trouble with doctors,' Madeleine said carefully. 'They only see you as a medical problem, not as a person.'

'Exactly.' Jordan gave a wry, twisted grin. 'Mr Brown the appendix, Mrs Jones the gall-bladder, Mr Sumner the compound fracture. It sounds like some sick sort of Happy Families, doesn't it?'

'Just like that.'

Madeleine tried hard to keep her voice light, so as not to let him know that she had caught the one revealing word. Compound fracture, he had said, which made his injury not the simple, clean break he had implied at first.

'And Miss Crawford the foot,' she continued obliquely, wondering if he would follow her.

He did. 'You, too? What happened?'

'I got in my father's way when he was laying some concrete slabs for a path. One of them landed right on my foot. It was a long time ago—I was fourteen at the time.'

But not so long ago that she couldn't remember with vivid clarity that moment of stunned shock before the pain actually began, and the seemingly endless frustration of having every movement hampered by the clumsy plaster cast.

'I remember I was hobbling around for ages in plaster. I nearly went crazy. So you see——' A quick sidelong glance at Jordan's face checked to see if he would accept this. 'I do know something of how it feels.'

But he wasn't going to follow her down that path. The silvery eyes were carefully bland and unrevealing, his smile a mere flicker across his face.

'Well, that's all past history now. The plaster's been off for a while and they tell me it's getting stronger every day.'

'When will you be able to get back to normal completely—do things like driving?'

'I'm told I'll be able to *drive* very soon.'

He'd been careful, but not quite careful enough. Madeleine wondered if he knew just how much he gave away by such small things. He hadn't been able to obliterate the bitterness from his voice completely on the words 'they tell me', and 'drive' had had an undertone of emphasis that dismissed that activity as the last thing he was interested in doing.

'Your father must have felt terrible afterwards, if he dropped the stone on your foot.'

Diversionary tactics—let's talk about *you*. Oh well, if that was the way he wanted it . . .

'If I remember rightly, he swore at me and called me every name under the sun for getting in his way.' Madeleine's smile was hard. 'Afterwards, I think he was quite pleased to be given an excuse not to finish the job. He hated working in the garden or the house—in fact, he hated being at home, full stop. He moved out very soon after that.'

Carefully Madeleine moved out to overtake a cyclist, concentrating hard on what she was doing in order to suppress the nagging ache that could still surface, even after all this time.

'Your parents are divorced?'

'Separated.' The car swung smoothly back to the side of the road. 'They never got round to making it legal.' Her voice shook slightly on the words, because now other memories were surfacing, ones not quite so distant and much harder to handle.

'And what about you?'

'Me?' Because she had expected the usual polite, 'I'm sorry', followed by a careful change of subject, Jordan's question put her at a loss.

'How do you feel about it?'

'Oh, it was all a long time ago—like the injury to my foot.'

'Not quite long enough,' Jordan stated firmly.

'Time heals.' She tried for flippancy, but didn't quite succeed.

'But not completely—not in your case,' Jordan persisted, and with a faint sigh Madeleine gave up trying to pretend.

'No,' she said softly. Just as the bones in her foot, broken all those years ago, could sometimes catch her up short with a sudden ache, so too could the thought of her father, so inextricably mixed with the memory of that injury, still stab at her when she least expected it.

'Did he leave when your foot was still in plaster?'

The accuracy of that inspired guess had Madeleine's hands tightening around the wheel as she nodded.

'You must have felt terribly betrayed.'

'Yes.' Still stunned by his perceptiveness, it was all she could manage. She *had* felt betrayed, had hated her father for walking out at a time when she had felt so particularly vulnerable. So she had cut herself off from him, refusing ever to visit him, and then...

'You can always tell me to get lost, you know,' Jordan said quietly. Then he added, with a touch of dryness, 'Metaphorically, I mean. I doubt if I'd get very far if you abandoned me here—I don't even know where we are.'

'The village we've just passed through is Enderby. Northcote is a couple of miles down this road, and the Hall itself is perhaps a mile and a half beyond that—and, no, I don't mind talking about my father, really I don't. Most of the time I don't think about it any more, but then something triggers off a memory and it all comes bubbling up to the surface again.'

'The mucking-out syndrome.' Jordan nodded.

'The what?'

'Sometimes the bad bits of the past, the unhappy memories, pile up in your mind like soiled bedding in a horse's stall—and the only way to stop them fouling up your life is to clear them all out—like mucking-out a stable.'

'Oh, I see. Yes, that does describe it pretty well.'

She had temporarily forgotten that Jordan's life revolved around horses and stables. With his injured leg it must be quite some time since he had been able to ride; he must find that intensely frustrating. Perhaps that was what the subtle emphasis on the word 'drive' had hidden earlier.

Beside her, Jordan shifted slightly in his seat and, without looking at him, she sensed that his leg was troubling him but he was too polite or too proud to say so.

'Would you like some coffee?' she asked, to make things easy for him. 'I packed a flask—we could park here, where it's quiet, if you like.'

In spite of the bright sunshine it was still very cool, hardly the weather for a picnic, and Madeleine was glad of her red and black checked wool jacket as she cupped her hands around the top of the thermos flask, savouring the tang of the hot coffee. The jacket was far from new and so were the denim jeans and red polo-necked sweater she wore with it but, as she had learned to her cost on one early occasion—when she had had to investigate two huge, filthy attics and had ruined a rather expensive cream suit in the process—hunting round sale rooms or the interiors of old houses was often dusty, dirty work. So she had dressed for practicality rather than glamour, pulling her dark hair back in a long ponytail that fell half-way down her back.

The Mini's passenger door stood open, and if she looked in the rear-view mirror she could see Jordan fifty yards or so down the road where he had walked, coffee-cup in hand, to ease the stiffness in his leg after having sat in a cramped space for so long. In the dark jacket and trousers, his shoulders hunched against the wind, he looked a lonely, isolated figure, the sight of him reminding her of how swiftly he had cut her off when she had ventured just a few steps too close—which made it all the more strange that so soon afterwards *she* had been the one who had opened up to him.

Frowning, Madeleine considered the dark figure in the mirror. It was a long time since she had even mentioned her father to anyone. Her mother never spoke about him; the marriage was a closed book as far as she was concerned; and her sisters were absorbed in their own lives, the unhappy memories of the past tacitly avoided by all of them. In fact, if she had been asked, Madeleine would have said that it was all behind her too, but, by mentioning her accident in an attempt to show Jordan that in some small way she did understand the frustration of waiting for broken bones to heal, she had dug deeper than she had meant to and found that the memories were not as safely buried as she had thought. And she hadn't been able to share all of it. She wondered if she would ever be truly healed until she did.

What had Jordan called it? The mucking-out syndrome... Her frown deepened as she recalled his swift changing of the subject, his laconic and unenlightening mention of his accident and his careful avoidance of any full account of how he had come by his injury. A shiver that had nothing to do with the cold crept down her spine. Just what memories were piling up in *his* mind? she wondered.

He had turned now and was coming towards the car. Fearful that he might realise she had been watching him, Madeleine hastily dropped her eyes to stare at the toes of her black boots. That limp was worse than she had realised; she wondered if it would ever completely vanish. Perhaps he would be left with a noticeable unevenness for the rest of his life. She found the thought upsetting, like the idea of a bird with a broken wing. The compact strength of Jordan's body, the controlled power of trained muscle that even the bulky jacket couldn't disguise should be matched with an easy, lithe grace of movement, not this stiff dragging of one leg.

As the car moved forward smoothly Madeleine glanced at her watch, then shook her wrist irritatedly.

'The wretched thing's stopped! What time is it?'

Jordan consulted a workmanlike, leather-strapped watch on his own wrist. 'Eleven-fifteen.'

She had thought it was later than that. Driving through the quiet lanes with Jordan at her side had a strange familiarity. It was exactly twenty-four hours since she had first met Jordan, and yet in some strange way she already felt as if she had never not known him.

But at the same time she had to admit that she was no closer to really knowing Jordan than she had been when she met him the day before. He had told her so little about himself, and had positively discouraged any attempt on her part to probe any deeper into the circumstances of his accident—which made this strange feeling of familiarity all the more puzzling.

'I really appreciate your doing this,' Jordan said quietly. 'Believe me, I don't usually approach young women I've only just met and ask such favours of them, but I'd been wondering how the hell I could get to Northcote without an Evensleigh or two in attendance.' The glance he shot at Madeleine was filled with a wry irony. 'Rupert's every bit as thick-skinned as his brother, and neither of them can understand that not everyone wants to do everything in a crowd.'

'We all need a little space,' Madeleine agreed, thinking back over years of sharing with her sisters, remembering the overwhelming need to be alone sometimes. 'I used to lock myself in the bathroom with a book when I was younger.'

Jordan gave a convulsive snort of laughter. 'I bet that made you popular!'

'It did! My sisters would bang on the door to tell me to hurry up and I'd just run the water to pretend I was having a bath, and carry on reading. But I know what you mean about Rupert and Peter. They're like schoolboys, always in a gang.'

Jordan nodded agreement. 'And I needed to look at Northcote again on my own. Houses have an atmosphere that tell you if they're right or not, but you need peace to sense it. If I'm going to invest everything I have in Northcote, I have to be sure.'

And that was something Madeleine understood. When they had been looking for premises in which to open the antiques shop, her mother had despaired of the way she had turned down more than one possible opening because the vibrations weren't right. But, not wanting to break Jordan's train of thought, she let it pass without comment, just as she clamped her mouth shut on the questions she wanted to ask about why he wanted to buy Northcote, what he planned to do with the house. For the first time, Jordan had started to open up to her and she didn't want to spoil things with a distracting question that might cause him to withdraw from her once again.

'I had no idea how I was going to get to the Hall,' Jordan was saying. 'I didn't know anyone locally except the Evensleighs—but then you said you were planning to drive out here today and it seemed too good an opportunity to miss. I just had to hope you wouldn't mind my asking.'

'I didn't,' Madeleine told him honestly, but her tone was abstracted, her thoughts elsewhere. She was remembering the feeling she had had yesterday morning, that strange sense of anticipation and excitement that had led to her impulsive offer to take her mother's place at the antiques fair. If she hadn't done that, she would never have met Jordan Sumner and would now be driving to Northcote on her own as she had originally planned.

It was impossible not to think that in some way it had all been meant, that she had been fated to meet Jordan, meant to make this journey with him. There was no rational explanation for it, but some things had no part in logical or rational deduction, they had a law all of their own. All she could do was let that destiny run its course, and then maybe she would find out exactly why the Fates had brought her and Jordan together like this.

CHAPTER THREE

As a result of several years' experience in such matters, Madeleine had a tried and tested routine that she followed at every auction preview or house sale she attended. She started with a swift survey of every room, then moved on to a slower, more intensive study of individual objects, checking them for flaws and jotting down in a notebook a possible price, higher than which she was not prepared to go. After that she found a quiet corner in which to check over her notes and add up the total expenditure she had detailed. If it was within her budget she could leave, knowing she was prepared for the battle of the auction itself the next day. If she had gone over her limit then she had one more survey to complete, reconsidering any items she was unsure of and arranging them in an order of importance, the things she most wanted first.

But now, with Jordan to consider as well as herself, she couldn't just launch into the familiar routine, knowing that once the instinct for hunting out bargains caught her up she would become totally absorbed, oblivious to anyone or anything else. Once out of the sunshine and inside the cool, shady main hall, she hesitated, glancing uncertainly at the man beside her.

'Where do you want to start?' she asked. 'Inside or out? I could——' She broke off as Jordan raised his hand to silence her.

'You don't have to dance attendance on me, Miss Crawford,' he said. 'I'm sure you have plenty you want to look at, and I'll be quite happy just to wander around at my own pace. Why don't we go our separate ways and meet up again later?'

He'd done it again, Madeleine thought to herself. His tone had been perfectly polite, his suggestion thoroughly reasonable, but all the same he had managed to inject a hint of dismissal, almost of rejection into the words. Just as he had warned her off from enquiring too closely into his private life earlier, so now he was deliberately putting a distance between them, taking several steps away from her mentally, and that carefully formal 'Miss Crawford' showed that he felt nothing of that strange sense of familiarity that she had experienced during the journey to Northcote.

'I think an hour and a half should be long enough for me to see everything I want,' she said, thankful that her voice betrayed nothing of her unsettled thoughts. 'We could meet back here at about half-past one.'

'Suits me,' was Jordan's laconic response. He was already turning away, but stilled as Madeleine spoke again.

'By the way,' she said impulsively. 'Not Miss Crawford, please. My name's Madeleine.'

A cool nod of acceptance was Jordan's only response, and Madeleine admitted to a pang of disappointment as she watched him move away. Still, what had she expected? she asked herself. That careful control was so rigidly imposed it seemed impossible that it would ever break—and yet it had cracked; in the car on the way to the Hall some real emotion had showed through very briefly when he had talked about his damaged leg. But he had very soon covered it up, steering the conversation carefully on to the subject of herself. Was it just with her that he was so reticent? Or did he react like this with everyone else?

With a faint sigh, Madeleine pushed all thoughts of Jordan to the back of her mind and forced herself to concentrate on the job she had come to the Hall to do. As always, she was very soon caught up in the thrill of an experience that had always seemed like a treasure hunt, becoming completely unaware of the passage of time, and only surfacing when the time for her meeting with Jordan was well past. Her conscience pricking her at having kept him waiting so long, she hurried to the hall, expecting to find that he had grown impatient and irritable in the intervening period.

Instead she found him sitting on the carved stone staircase, the sunlight that filtered through the tall, stained glass window behind him casting coloured shadows of red, blue and green over his face and hair and tinting them in an unearthly, surrealistic way, the sight bringing her to a halt in the doorway to stand silently watching him, fascinated by what she saw.

With his complete stillness and sombre clothing, the strong, narrow hands clasped lightly in his lap and that high-boned, finely carved face set in an expression of austere reflection, Jordan might have been taken for the ghost of some monk who had visited the Hall in the sixteenth century when it had first been built, his private meditations holding him unmoving and silent as if carved from stone. What thoughts lay behind that pale and remote mask? Madeleine wondered. Not happy ones, clearly, to judge by the stern set of that hard mouth, the touch of red and white in the clasped hands, that spoke of an unnatural pressure of one against the other. She felt her heart twist in sympathy in the same moment that she acknowledged that she would probably never find out; Jordan seemed so determined to keep the distance he had imposed between them.

But she must have moved or made some sound that Jordan caught, for suddenly the smoky eyes lifted from their contemplation of the stone-flagged floor, and the coloured lights shifted and broke as he got to his feet. His mouth curved into a swift, brief smile of welcome, but Madeleine saw the way that smile did not reach his eyes and she experienced a sudden stabbing pain of loss that, when it receded, left behind a dull, nagging ache that she found difficult to bear.

'Hi.' Jordan's tone was easy and light, with no evidence of the rigid, impenetrable barriers Madeleine could almost see behind his misty eyes. 'And my name's Jordan,' he went on, in an uncanny continuation of the conversation they had had at parting, as if the two hours in between had not existed.

'I'm sorry I'm late,' Madeleine mumbled, disconcerted by his affable mood, when she had seen that withdrawal in his eyes only moments before. But Jordan did not appear to notice her momentary disorientation.

'Don't worry about it. I was glad of the chance to sit quietly and think. Did you find anything interesting?'

That was a question guaranteed to lighten her mood. 'Oh, yes!' Madeleine hugged her notebook against her chest, an uncontrollable smile wreathing her face at the memory of the delightful time she had just spent. 'There's the most amazing collection of Gossware—dozens of tiny pieces—animals, jugs, cottages—there's even a lovely little sedan chair with a coat of arms on its roof. And in the same cupboard there was an almost complete set of Commemorative beakers and plates.'

'Do you just go for the small things—china and such?' Jordan asked as they moved towards the door.

'Oh no! We sell furniture as well, but that's Mother's department. The bric-a-brac sort of thing goes best at fairs, of course. I know a collector who'd just *kill* for a beautiful sampler I saw.'

'Sampler?' Jordan frowned his incomprehension.

'Embroidery,' Madeleine explained. 'Children used to learn to sew by embroidering their name, the date and some verses from the Bible, surrounded by designs worked in different coloured thread. Some are terribly complicated and done by very young children.' She swung round suddenly to face him. 'Can you imagine being stuck inside embroidering at *seven*?'

'No.' Jordan looked disconcerted by her vehemence. 'I have to admit I can't.'

But there was a sudden bleakness about his face that made Madeleine recall the bitterness with which he had spoken of the weeks he had spent in hospital. She could almost see the sterile whiteness of a hospital ward in his mind, sense the burning frustration he had felt at being incarcerated inside. To a man who was used to the freedom of the outdoors it must have been his own private hell on earth.

Remembering the startling attractiveness of the smile he used so sparingly, she wished she could wipe the hard, controlled expression from his face; its rigidity had a repelling quality about it. But when he smiled the transformation made Peter's or Rupert's good looks fade into showy insignificance.

They were out in the drive now, and Jordan turned back to face the house, his eyes narrowed against the sun as he surveyed the tall, grey stone building with the wide bay windows on either side of the door.

'Tell me about this place, Madeleine,' he said suddenly. 'Do you know its history?'

'Do I know it?' Madeleine laughed. 'You're talking to the girl who ran a Local History course for three years.' She needed no further urging to launch herself on one of her most abiding interests. 'This building dates back to 1857, when the Hall was sold to the Carlton family, but there was a house here long before that. In fact, you can still see the foundations of the original Elizabethan hall over here.'

Caught up in her own enthusiasm, she led the way across the lawns and, talking all the time, took Jordan on a guided tour of the grounds, through the rose garden, past the summer house and round to the stables at the back of the house.

'Northcote was sold in 1835 and the new owners, the Carltons, built the present hall. During the war it was let to the War Office—they used it to house Italian prisoners-of-war.' Madeleine slanted a laughing glance at Jordan. 'That's why you get some very dark-haired, dark-eyed locals. And, well, that's about it. Did you want to look at the stables?'

'I've seen them. They were the first thing I looked at.'

Of course! She had forgotten, once more, that his life centred around horses. Jordan was so very different from Peter and Rupert that she found it hard to think of him as a member of the 'horsy set'.

'It was the stables that attracted me to this place at first.' Jordan's tone had warmed with a hint of enthusiasm. 'There are plenty of other houses that offered the right sort of accommodation, but Northcote has the edge over them when it comes to provision for the horses. They'll be very comfortable here.'

Something about his words caught on Madeleine's nerves, jarring uncomfortably. He spoke as if the horses were his first, his only concern.

'And what about you?' she asked impetuously. 'Could you be happy here?'

She realised it was a mistake as soon as she spoke the words. During the walk around the grounds she had relaxed in Jordan's company, forgetting that careful restraint she had been so aware of at first, but now a swift alteration in his expression, a sudden coldness in his eyes as they glowed silver in the sunlight, brought her up sharp against the fact that she had somehow overstepped the invisible boundaries he drew around his privacy.

'I think you should buy it.' She tried a smile to lighten the atmosphere that had descended so swiftly. 'It seems right for you—you look as if you belong here.'

'Do you think so?' The smile hadn't worked. His voice was sharp and cold, no answering smile lightening his face. But now that she was looking at him more closely Madeleine saw the greyish tinge to his skin, the bruised look under his eyes.

'Are you all right?' she asked sharply, her conscience reproving her uncomfortably for the way she had been absorbed in her private local history lesson, forgetful of his injured leg. He looked drawn, the grey eyes dull and clouded, the lines scored down the side of his nose and mouth etched harshly in the sharp light of the clear spring sun, his lips just a tight, thin line. 'Jordan, what is it?'

Instinctively she reached out a hand to him, but he repelled it with a violent gesture.

'Don't fuss!' he snapped harshly.

'But I wish you'd let me help.'

Don't take it personally, she told herself, remembering how she had thought him the sort of man who would not accept sympathy easily. All the same, his rejection of her concern stung painfully, sharpening her voice as she added, 'Don't you think you should sit down?'

'Madeleine, I said—I'm sorry.'

The switch of mood and expression came so suddenly that Madeleine actually lifted a hand to rub at her temple to clear the confusion in her mind. One moment Jordan's eyes had blazed with cold hostility, every taut muscle in his body declaring his antagonism and an unspoken warning to keep away, the next it was as if a different man had taken his place, the black cloud of anger slipping away from his face to be replaced by an apologetic smile.

'I *am* sorry.'

Madeleine wondered if he was aware of how much he was giving away of what this new-found control was costing him. His voice was carefully polite, and the smile almost succeeded, but the tension in his shoulders, the tightly clenched hands at his sides, and an empty blankness about his eyes betrayed him to anyone who bothered to look closely.

He might force his mouth into a smile, pitch his voice at just the right level, but the rigidly unnatural control hid feelings of anger and pain that communicated themselves to her on a much more sensitive level than that of speech.

'I'm sorry,' Jordan said again, his voice just a tiny fraction more relaxed than before. 'Sometimes I forget about this damn leg until I find I've done too much.' A second attempt at a smile flashed on and off like a neon sign but, instead of reassuring as it was meant to, it simply reinforced Madeleine's conviction that there was more to his reaction than a simple physical tiredness. 'And it wouldn't help to sit down—if I did I might never get up again.'

If that was all he was going to let her know, then all she could do was follow his lead.

'We'd better go back to the car.' It came out unevenly; not possessing Jordan's ruthless control, Madeleine couldn't impose a lightness she wasn't feeling on her voice, and she was still smarting from his violent rejection of her gesture of sympathy.

She felt as if there were two men before her, the Jordan he let her see and the other, darker, hidden person that her instincts told her went far deeper than the veneer of casual friendliness he had shown until now. Sensing that Jordan would react angrily to any hint that she had seen the dark shadows behind the face he let her see, she directed her words at the public Jordan, struggling to pretend that she didn't know the private one existed.

'Can you walk to the car park, or shall I bring the Mini round here?'

'There's no need for that.' Jordan flashed that swift on-and-off smile at her worried face, with rather more conviction this time. 'I might be a little slow, but I always get there in the end.'

'A little slow', Madeleine soon learned, was a careful understatement. The walk back to the car seemed to take for ever and by the time they reached the black Mini Jordan was breathing harshly, the sheen of sweat glistening on his face silent evidence of how much the journey had taken out of him. He hadn't spoken a word since they'd left the stables and, respecting his need to keep silent, Madeleine walked wordlessly at his side, preoccupied with puzzling over the two distinct sides to his character, particularly the one only vaguely glimpsed behind the carefully controlled public face.

What dark shadow hung over Jordan's life, making him react in this way? She found herself considering her earlier feeling of familiarity with him, almost laughing out loud at her own naïveté in thinking any such thing. Jordan was a complete stranger, she knew nothing about him at all and, from the evidence of his behaviour, that was exactly how he wanted it to be.

'Are you aware of the time?' Jordan's voice broke in on her thoughts. He was leaning against the car, his breathing steadier now, a touch of colour returning to his face. 'It's after three,' he added, a smile curling his lips as Madeleine cast a furious glance at her still inaccurate watch. 'Which rather makes nonsense of what I was about to suggest.'

'And what was that?' Madeleine's fingers were busy moving the hands of her watch to the correct position. She needed something to distract her because that more natural smile, although it was only a shadow of the stunningly attractive one she had seen the day before, had made her heart lurch disturbingly into a beat that set her pulse racing.

'I had intended to offer you lunch to thank you for your kindness in bringing me here today.'

'Oh, there's no need for that!' The words came out unevenly, that accelerated beat of her heart leaving her slightly breathless. 'I told you—I was coming here anyway. You don't have to feel obliged to——'

'I don't feel *obliged* to do anything,' Jordan put in sharply. 'I wanted to ask you.'

'And I'd have liked to be able to accept,' Madeleine responded honestly. 'But I doubt if we'll find anywhere open now.' Regret crept into her voice. In spite of the tensions that had sometimes marred the morning, she had enjoyed being with Jordan and would have liked to continue the discovery of his complex character over lunch.

'Well, perhaps I could change the invitation to one for dinner this evening?'

'I'd like that very much!'

Madeleine smiled her pleasure straight into Jordan's eyes, surprising an answering gleam of response in their cloudy depths, the swift lifting of her heart telling her that she wanted this more than she had realised, and the thought that Jordan too wanted their time together to continue to put a lilt of happiness into her voice as she went on, 'But we'll starve if we don't have something to eat before then. If you don't mind taking pot luck you're welcome to come back and have lunch—or, rather, high tea—with me. I've no idea what's in the larder, Mother was going to visit one of my sisters this afternoon so she won't have prepared anything, but if you don't mind something quick and easy...'

Suddenly aware of how her tongue was running away with her, and uncertain how he would take her enthusiasm, she faltered awkwardly.

'Or—are you expected back at the Manor?' she finished lamely.

Jordan's shrug dismissed the Manor and the Evensleigh brothers along with it.

'Mr and Mrs Evensleigh are away for the weekend. And I told Rupert and Peter to expect me when they saw me.'

The edge to his voice on the two names reminded Madeleine of her suspicions that things weren't quite as friendly at the Manor as Peter had tried to lead her to believe.

'You don't like Peter and Rupert, do you?'

The cynical twist to Jordan's mouth was answer enough, and she didn't need his murmured, 'We tolerate each other,' to tell her how he felt.

'So why are you staying there?' she persisted, curiosity getting the better of her innate caution about asking him personal questions.

For a moment she thought he wasn't going to answer her, as those light eyes met her blue ones in a look she was coming to recognise all too well; all emotion blanked out, the steel doors well in place, smooth and impenetrable, with sharp spikes at the top to catch anyone foolhardy enough to try to scale them.

'Necessity,' he said curtly, then, apparently reconsidering, added unexpectedly, 'I needed to get away for a while—and I was looking for a place to buy. Mary Evensleigh is an old friend of my mother—they were at school together—so when I heard that Northcote Hall was on the market it was only logical—and polite—that I should stay at the Manor while I looked it over. I don't know anyone else around here. Correction: I didn't until yesterday.'

This time Jordan's smile was genuine, unconstrained, the sort of smile he used so rarely, but when he did its effect was devastating, the lightning-swift transformation of his normally austere expression, the translucent gleam of his silver eyes hitting home with an impact that made Madeleine's breath catch in her throat as her own lips curved in an involuntary response.

It was impossible not to wonder just what lay behind that cryptic, 'I needed to get away for a while.' The harsh note in Jordan's voice told her that he hadn't meant simply that he needed a break from his work or to continue his convalescence, but she knew that now was not the time to ask. If she was ever to win Jordan round to opening up to her, confiding in her, telling her just what shadows of the past darkened his life, she would have to be very careful and very patient. But she would find that patience, she told herself, she was determined to, because that smile had taught her something. She found Jordan's understated sort of looks infinitely more attractive than Peter Evensleigh's flamboyant handsomeness and, in three years of knowing Peter, never once had she experienced one of those flashes of empathy that had sprung up between herself and Jordan on those rare occasions since she had first met him.

She still knew very little about him, he could be difficult to talk to, totally unpredictable, and at times, openly hostile, but she was drawn to him as she had never been to any other man in her life, and for now that was enough. The rest could come later, she told herself as she swung the car out of the drive and into Holtby Road. They had the rest of this afternoon and all the evening ahead of them—and she wasn't at all surprised to find herself anticipating that time with a swift and powerful surge of pleasure.

CHAPTER FOUR

'I LIKE this house. Did you say you lived here with your mother?' Jordan asked, swinging round from the window where he had been looking out at the small back garden. 'Just your mother?' he continued in response to Madeleine's nod of agreement. 'You said something about sisters.'

'That's right—but none of them live at home any more. Nancy and Miriam are——'

'Hey, hang on!' Jordan put up a hand to stop her. 'How many sisters do you have?'

A mischievous smile played over Madeleine's lips. 'Four,' she declared with some pride. 'Nancy, Miriam, Joan and Pat.'

'Five daughters—six women altogether! No wonder your father felt out of it! No, I'm sorry—I had no right to say that.'

'It's all right,' Madeleine assured him with a smile. 'As a matter of fact, I've often wondered if that was how he felt. My father was very much a man's man, the type who liked to be one of the boys. I don't think he really understood women and, looking back, I can see that we were all very close—a sort of feminine clique with him on the outside.'

'What did he do?'

'His job, you mean? He taught physical education at the local comprehensive. Sport was his life really. Football, rugby, you name it, he played it. Mother's quite the opposite, but in the early days she used to go to matches to watch Dad play. But she hated it, really, and when the first baby came along she was glad of an excuse not to bother any more... I think that was when they started to drift apart. My father was always out playing football or in the pub with his mates, and Mum was left at home with all of us. There were so many rows and then, when I was fourteen, he left.'

'Earlier you said your parents were separated, but now you're talking of your father in the past.'

Madeleine flinched mentally. Jordan was too quick, too perceptive for comfort sometimes.

'He died five years ago when I was at university.'

It was a flat little statement that revealed nothing of the way she had felt when the news had reached her. Jordan waited quietly, not saying a word, leaving her to go on in her own time if she wanted to and, strangely, his silence was more encouraging than if he had actually spoken. It had been the same in the car on the way to Northcote, Madeleine reflected. There was something about him that drew the truth from her.

'I hated him for leaving us, for abandoning us in that way, so I never saw him again, never spoke to him, even though he only moved to the next village. I thought I could never forgive him for what he'd done. Then, when I went to university, I started to see things differently. I realised how hard he must have found it to have given up his dreams as he did. He'd always wanted to be a professional footballer, but he met Mother when he was only nineteen and switched to the idea of teaching instead because it was safer, a regular income to support a family.'

Madeleine sighed, her blue eyes clouding at the memories she was recalling.

'I came to see how isolated he must have felt without anyone to share his interests, and I was determined to put things right. I resolved that when I got home at Christmas I would go and see him, talk to him, make some effort to heal the breach that had opened up between us since he'd left—but it was too late, I never got the chance.' Her voice weakened, becoming just a thin thread of sound.' One morning I got a phone call from my uncle to say that my father had had a heart attack and died during the night—he was only fifty-three.'

Madeleine swallowed hard. Tears stung her eyes and she blinked furiously to drive them back.

'Hey,' Jordan's voice was soft and low, 'I didn't mean to rake up bad memories.'

'You didn't.' Madeleine's smile came wanly. 'I did the raking up myself.'

'But I asked the questions.'

Yes, he'd asked the questions, and Madeleine was still wondering exactly what it was about this man that made her open up to him like this. Never before had she admitted to anyone, not even her mother, how guilty she had felt about the distance that had come between herself and her father, but somehow, with this stranger, it had all come pouring out. She felt better for having said it, calmer and somehow refreshed. It was like a new beginning. She rubbed at her eyes, brushing away the tears.

'Madeleine?' Concern sounded in Jordan's voice, then an arm was slung casually around her shoulders, drawing her closer, and Jordan's warm, hard hand rubbed her cheek in an oddly awkward gesture of comfort, as if he was somehow unsure of her response. Did he think she would panic simply because he had touched her?

Accustomed to Peter's pushy approaches, Madeleine found that slight hesitancy curiously touching. She had no intention of rejecting Jordan's embrace, she felt warm and safe in his arms, like being enclosed in a soft, cosy blanket, and she appreciated his gesture for what it was, the action of one friend offering comfort to another. Experimentally she cuddled closer, resting her head on the soft cotton of his shirt.

Immediately her feelings changed completely, as a totally different feeling swept through her, one that set her heart pounding and made her legs tremble beneath her. Her breathing quickened, becoming swift and shallow as every nerve-end in her body came tingling alive to the scent and feel of Jordan's hard body so close to her. Her skin glowed as if it was bathed in warm sunlight and the one thought that filled her mind was that she desperately wanted Jordan to kiss her. She had even lifted her head slightly in anticipation when, with a sudden, jarring shock, she became aware of his reaction.

She could hear the change in the rate of Jordan's heartbeat beneath her cheek, sense a new tension in the firm muscles of the arm around her shoulder, and knew in a moment of blinding, shocking clarity that it wasn't *her* reaction he was concerned about—it was his own! *He* was holding back, fighting the impulse that had made him put his arm round her with all his strength. She was as close to him as it was possible to be, every inch of her body touching the compact strength of his, but the rigid restraint Jordan was imposing on himself meant that they might as well have been at the opposite sides of the room.

He doesn't want this! The realisation made her lift her head in distress, the golden glow that had filled her fading swiftly, leaving her feeling empty and shaken, a dull, nagging ache of loss starting up deep inside her. She had reacted instinctively, responding to her feelings on the simplest, most basic level, but Jordan had not felt that way at all and his rejection of her stabbed like a white-hot knife. Unable to look at him, she eased herself away from his side, and the speed with which he released her added unbearably to her sense of desolation.

'Thanks.' It was an awkward murmur as she struggled to get her thoughts back into some order. How could she have misread the situation so completely? She had been at the mercy of that instinctive attraction she had felt towards him from the very start, a force so strong that it had led her to forget that deliberate distance Jordan had been so careful to establish between them. Hesitantly she lifted her eyes to Jordan's, trying to read his thoughts in them, but they were hooded, impenetrable, those steel doors firmly in place, repelling any attempt to probe into what he really felt.

'Would you like some more coffee?' she asked, seizing on practicalities in an attempt to defuse the tension she had felt in him. 'And shouldn't you be sitting down? You ought to rest that leg of yours.'

'Coffee would be nice.' Jordan's voice was as carefully schooled as his face, giving nothing away, and he moved to a chair obediently but somehow automatically, as if he had heard what she had said and was acting on it without thinking, his mind preoccupied with other, more private matters.

'I don't usually crack up like that.' Madeleine concentrated hard on the coffee she was pouring, her hand shaking very slightly as she tried to squash down that ache of loss that still tormented her. 'It's just that it's been a long time since I talked to anyone about my dad—it sort of took me unawares.'

'I'm glad you felt you could talk to me.' Jordan seemed to have emerged from his abstracted mood; his voice sounded clearer and his eyes had lost some of their opaque, withdrawn look.

'I don't usually confide in people I've just met,' Madeleine admitted, trying to centre her thoughts on that wonderfully soothing sense of friendship she had felt in Jordan's arms in an attempt to forget what had happened afterwards. 'But somehow I don't feel as if you are a stranger. I feel——' She faltered awkwardly as Jordan turned a direct, searching glance on her face.

'Tell me about yourself, Madeleine,' he said quietly. 'If we're going to be friends, I'd like to know more about you.'

Friends. Madeleine's heart leapt in delight at Jordan's use of the word, her pleasure easing some of the pain of his earlier withdrawal. It was a tiny step forward, and she hadn't known until he had said it how much she had wanted him to feel that too.

'Start at the beginning,' Jordan was saying. 'What were you like as a child?'

'But that's not fair!' Madeleine protested lightly, the brief, charming smile that had accompanied his words giving her the encouragement she needed to try to change the mood of the moment. 'You already know about my family and what I do. You're several steps ahead of me, so it's your turn now.'

She expected—and got—that steel-shuttered look but, with that hopeful 'friends' still ringing in her ears, she refused to let it disconcert her or wipe the smile from her face.

'Your name, I know,' she continued blithely, determined not to let him see that she had even noticed his withdrawal. 'So that's one.' She ticked off the point on her fingers. 'Two—age?' She paused expectantly.

'Thirty-two.' The lack of hesitation in his answer, and the way his mouth quirked up at one corner told her she was winning, though his eyes were still carefully blanked off and she felt as if she was being watched to make sure she didn't get too close.

'So old?' She affected astonishment, her eyebrows shooting up, and saw his slight relaxation before she heard his indignant laugh.

'Not so very ancient, young madam! You may have noticed that *I* was polite enough to avoid asking *your* age.'

'One never asks a lady her age,' Madeleine declared haughtily. 'But if you're clever you can work it out from the clues I've given you.'

Jordan's eyes narrowed thoughtfully. 'You mentioned university, five years ago... Twenty-four?' he hazarded.

'You *have* been listening! I *am* twenty-four, but not for much longer.'

'When will you be twenty-five?'

'May—hey, that's cheating! You got an extra fact out of me!'

Jordan's grin was wide, spontaneous and, Madeleine was relieved to see, completely unshadowed, but she still had the feeling she was walking on eggs, treading very carefully, testing the ground with each move, praying she did nothing to destroy the mood she had tried to build up by driving him to withdraw from her again.

'Will it even the score if I tell you I'll be thirty-three in November? On the twenty-fifth, to be precise.'

'It might,' Madeleine conceded. 'So you're Sagittarius, are you? Interesting, so's Nancy. Now, where was I? Oh, yes—family?'

'The usual two parents, one sister, one brother.'

'Older or younger?'

'My sister's older, and Mick's three years younger.'

'So you come in the middle—and you know what they say about middle children——'

'No.' Jordan took a sip of his coffee, watching her over the top of his cup. 'What do they say?'

'Determined, independent—loners, in fact—and often difficult. Are you like that?'

But Jordan was not to be drawn. 'I think we're even now, so I get to ask some questions.'

'Oh, but——' Madeleine was about to protest that he hadn't told her anything yet, there was so much she wanted to know about him, but she was well aware that the scales could swing against her at any moment and so decided it was better to compromise. 'We'll take it in turns, one question each.' Her expression became mischievous. 'Things like—what's your favourite food?'

'Cheat!' Jordan growled in mock reproach, but he answered the question anyway. 'Home-baked wholemeal bread with an unhealthy amount of butter on it, or anything Italian.' He grinned as Madeleine nodded enthusiastic agreement. 'Favourite drink?'

'Non-alcoholic—coffee; alcoholic—white Lambrusco.'

'Red,' Jordan countered.

'*White*. And it's my turn. Favourite author?'

'Dickens. You?'

'Emily Brontë—but they're both nineteenth century, so I'll let you have that. Was that a question?'

'Not on your life! Music?'

Madeleine wrinkled her nose thoughtfully. 'That's a hard one. I love Beethoven and Dylan—and almost anything in between. Oh, but I can't cope with jazz, it leaves me cold. You're not a jazz addict, are you?'

When Jordan shook his head, she sighed with relief.

'I once had a boyfriend who played nothing but Basie and Duke Ellington.' She grimaced at the memory.

'An ex-boyfriend?' Jordan asked and Madeleine nodded.

'Very ex! Our tastes in music were pretty typical of the whole relationship—it was all a big mistake. We were miles apart really, except in bed.'

Damn! How had that slipped out? Madeleine coloured as she heard what she had said. It sounded appallingly blasé, spoken so casually, making it sound as if she had had dozens of lovers, which was very far from the case. Viv had been the only one, at a time when she had sincerely believed herself in love with him, and there had been no one since. Cautiously she glanced at Jordan to see how he had taken her unguarded words. Grey eyes met blue without a hint of disapproval.

'I'm casting no stones,' Jordan said mildly. 'My own slate isn't exactly clean on such matters. I think I owe you an extra question.'

Because he had asked if Viv was her ex-boyfriend? Madeleine wondered. Or because she had answered a question he hadn't asked? For a second she allowed herself to consider what her response would have been if Jordan *had* asked if she was a virgin and, rather surprisingly, came up with the answer that she would have told him just the same. There was something about him that drew the truth from her.

'Madeleine?' Jordan prompted quietly.

'Oh—yes——' Disconcerted by her own thoughts, she hunted frantically for a question. 'Favourite sport? No, I know that already—horse-riding—eventing.'

One of those quick, light, electrifying glances flickered over her, and the silver eyes darkened with something that tugged sharply at her nerves, warning her of the need for caution.

'Peter,' Jordan said, the single word definite to the point of curtness.

He leaned forward to place his coffee-cup on the table, then folded his hands together and rested his chin on them. The slight movement drew Madeleine's eyes to the taut strength of his fingers and wrists, a strength that she now knew came from controlling powerful horses in difficult conditions, and a cold shiver ran down her spine at the memory of the touch of those hands on hers.

'But would you have known that if Peter hadn't told you?'

Madeleine didn't have to look at Jordan's face to know that the easy mood had changed and his guard was up again. Why did that matter so much? she wondered, but no answer presented itself and she knew a strong sense of relief that his question was an easy one to answer honestly.

'No, I have to admit I'm completely ignorant where horses are concerned. As a matter of fact, when Peter talked of Badminton I thought he meant the game—you know—rackets and shuttlecocks.'

Her shamefaced admission broke the tension swiftly. Jordan threw back his head and laughed aloud, and Madeleine found herself laughing with him. But underneath her amusement ran a thread of uncertainty. Just why should Jordan be concerned that she might know of his riding successes? If he was as good as Peter said, then surely he would have wanted her to know.

'Do you still ride?' she asked impulsively. Seeing his face change yet again, she knew that, forgetting his injury, she had blundered badly.

'Ask my doctor about that,' he said curtly, the coldness of his tone affecting her like a blow to her face, reminding her of that other, darker side to him that she had sensed earlier, and sending her into a hurried search for something to bring the conversation back to a safer topic.

'Favourite film?' she managed. She had forgotten whose turn it was, but it no longer seemed to matter.

'Play Misty for Me.' The title came harshly, and Madeleine was almost certain he had answered off the top of his head, saying the first thing that came into his mind; but at least he had responded and the ground felt slightly firmer beneath her feet. Luckily, the film he had mentioned was one she had seen on television very recently.

'It's a good film,' she said carefully. 'It had me on the edge of my seat—but I don't go for the Clint Eastwood type at all.'

'No?' Jordan looked surprised and intrigued. 'I thought most women fantasised over the tall, dark and handsome type.'

'Not me!' Some of Madeleine's confidence returned with the lightening of his expression. 'He reminds me too much of Peter Evensleigh—or, rather, the way Peter thinks of himself.'

She was rewarded by Jordan's laughter once more, this time a natural, warm chuckle that she could share without any doubts of her own.

'Poor Peter,' Jordan murmured drily. 'He thinks he has quite the opposite effect on you. You do know he's told everyone that you're going to be his partner at the Spring Ball?'

'He hasn't!' Madeleine groaned. 'I've tried being kind, I've tried telling him straight that I just don't want to go with him, but he won't listen. I don't know how I can make it any plainer.'

'You could always say you're going with someone else,' Jordan suggested off-handedly.

'Like whom?' Madeleine asked. As her mother was only too keen to point out, eligible young men didn't exactly grow on the trees around Holtby.

'Like me.'

'You!' It was so unexpected that Madeleine simply stared. Jordan's mouth twisted wryly.

'Has the idea so little appeal?' he asked on a note of irony. 'I realise that my dancing skills will be pretty limited, but I thought we got on rather well.'

'We do—but—I mean—will you still be here then?'

'Oh, yes.' The twist to Jordan's mouth became more pronounced. 'I'll still be here. In fact, if everything goes according to plan, I shall be living here permanently.'

'You're definitely going to buy the Hall, then?'

Jordan nodded silently. 'You should know that. You're the one who told me it was right before I'd quite decided for myself.'

There was a dark undertone to his voice, one that made her tense in her seat, as she was reminded once more of the way Jordan had often made it clear that there were parts of himself and his life that he wanted to keep hidden. She felt her nerves grow taut with the apprehension that was never far from the surface when she was with this man.

'I thought you could be happy there,' she said, her uncertainty making the words come out stiffly. Jordan's brows drew together as he caught the hesitancy in her voice.

'You don't approve?'

'Approve?' Madeleine was genuinely puzzled.

'I thought perhaps you might object to one man owning all that space, when there are others who have only tiny flats or no homes at all.'

'Oh, no! I don't think that at all. But you will rather rattle about in it, won't you?'

Jordan's grin, absent from his face since the conversation had taken this turn, surfaced again to Madeleine's overwhelming relief.

'I won't be on my own. At the last count there were five grooms, my brother and his wife, ten horses, two cats and a dog all planning to live with me—not to mention a couple of trainee stable-boys aged six and three—my nephews,' he added, seeing Madeleine's blank look.

'You're not just buying the Hall as a home, then?'

'Good lord, no! My finances aren't in the Evensleigh class at all. The idea is to turn it into a breeding and training stables, in partnership with my brother.'

'Your brother rides, too?'

A brief nod signified agreement. 'Mick concentrates on the show-jumping side.'

Jordan stretched lazily, tightening the hard muscles in his arms and shoulders, and drawing his dark shirt taut across his chest in a way that sent a prickle of awareness running down Madeleine's spine, as she recalled the sensations being held close against that chest had aroused in her earlier.

'It's getting late,' he said, 'and I promised you dinner—don't you want to get changed or something?'

Madeleine considered. It came as no surprise to find how reluctant she was to move. Jordan's frequent changes of mood made conversation with him hard work at times, but at last they seemed to have achieved a companionable mood that she didn't want to break even for the half an hour or so it would take her to wash and change. She was afraid that this tentative beginning might evaporate into thin air if she did, that she would come downstairs again and find that Jordan had retreated from her once more. Nor did she want to expose this fragile relationship to the bustle and noise of a busy restaurant. She felt greedy, selfish, wanting to keep it to herself for as long as she could.

'Do you really want to go out?' she asked with careful casualness. 'We could have dinner here—I could cook us something. I make an excellent lasagne,' she added enticingly, remembering how he had said he liked Italian food.

It was obvious that Jordan was tempted. Neither by a word nor any external sign had he made any reference to his damaged leg after that one brief admission of weakness at Northcote, but she was well aware of the relief with which he had slumped in a chair on their arrival at the house, and he had carefully kept all movement to a minimum since then. On the few occasions he had got to his feet, the jarring unevenness in his walk had seemed more pronounced than before and, if she guessed right, he was reluctant to walk any further than he had to.

'But dinner was to have been my way of saying thank you,' Jordan protested.

Madeleine waved aside his objection. 'I don't need thanks for the little I did. But if you're determined on it we can go out some other night. You see,' she went on with sudden inspiration, 'Peter told me that he and Rupert and Geraldine were planning on dining out in Holtby tonight—he asked me to go with them. If we went out, we'd almost certainly meet up with them.'

The expression on Jordan's face told her her dart had hit home. Feeling as he did about Rupert and Peter, she wondered how he coped, living at the Manor twenty-four hours a day.

'That would definitely not be the perfect end to a perfect day,' Jordan said firmly. 'Though I'd give a lot to see the expression on Peter's face if you walked in with me.'

'It would rather upset his lady-killer image,' Madeleine agreed, knowing that the decision had been made without either of them taking it.

But as she busied herself with the preparations for the meal Madeleine could not prevent her mind from going over and over the things Jordan had said. 'The perfect end to a perfect day.' It was a common phrase and he had used it lightly, jokingly. Would she be a fool to allow herself to hope that perhaps, in some small way, he had meant it, or would that just be laying herself open to another rejection like the one that had so devastated her earlier that afternoon?

CHAPTER FIVE

'You never gave me an answer to my question,' Jordan said obscurely when the meal was finished. They were lingering over the last of the wine beside the fire he had lit against the encroaching chill of the evening.

'Your question?' Madeleine frowned her confusion, thinking back.

There had been so many questions and answers throughout the time it had taken to prepare and eat the meal. The whole procedure had taken on something of the aspect of a game, one of them flinging 'Favourite...?' at the other when they thought of a question. It had all been light-hearted and fun, and she had relaxed completely, pushing away all thought of the dark moods that sometimes changed Jordan into that other disturbing and unpredictable stranger. But now she was at a loss to know which question Jordan meant. As far as she could remember, she had answered everything he had asked.

'Which question was that?'

Jordan considered the wine in his glass—white Lambrusco, Madeleine thought with a smile. He had conceded on that because it was the only bottle she had in the house, but had declared that when he took her out for dinner it would be red or nothing.

'I asked if you'd be my partner at the Ball,' he murmured nonchalantly, his eyes still on the bubbles that floated to the top of his glass.

'Oh!' Madeleine sat up with a jolt. 'I thought that was a joke.'

'A joke!' Jordan's eyes lifted to hers, widening in a pretence of shock. 'I was deadly serious,' he declared in a hurt voice, then ruined the effect by adding with a quiver of laughter in his voice, 'Like I said, I'd give anything to see Peter's face when he sees you with me.'

'That has to be the least flattering invitation I've ever received!' Madeleine spluttered indignantly.

'But will you accept it?' Jordan parried smoothly.

'Well, considering it's a choice between you and Peter, I suppose I shall have to,' Madeleine shot back, using flippancy to disguise the shake in her voice that came from her reaction to a sharp stab of something that felt disturbingly like disappointment deep inside her. She had no time to search her feelings for a reason for it, because a second later she was laughing at Jordan's exaggerated wince of pain.

'That was a bit below the belt! Would you have preferred it if I'd couched the invitation in more formal terms?'

Jordan placed his glass on the table and, leaning over to take her hand, looked straight into her eyes.

'Miss Crawford, I would be overjoyed if you would do me the honour of being my partner at the Spring Ball.'

'Mr Sumner, I would be delighted to accept your kind invitation.'

It was an effort to match Jordan's gracious tone, play-acting though it was. The sudden intimacy of the moment was doing strange things to Madeleine's pulse-rate, making it skip a beat and then start up again in double time.

'Idiot!' she laughed rather nervously. 'Of course I'll come!'

'Good.'

Jordan released her hand and turned away to pick up his glass once more. Madeleine was intensely grateful that his attention was directed elsewhere, as her smile wavered and then vanished completely under the impact of a second, stronger pain close to her heart, and this time there was no way of avoiding acknowledging the reason for it.

It was Jordan's indifference that hurt, the carelessness with which he had made the offer to be her partner at the ball and the flat, matter-of-fact way he had acknowledged her acceptance. Fool! Madeleine reproved herself angrily. What had she expected? That he would fall madly in love with her on sight? No, she hadn't hoped for anything like that, but all the same that stabbing pain told her that she *had* hoped for something more than he had given her.

Recalling the lift of her heart at Jordan's casual use of the word 'friends', Madeleine was forced to admit that in an unbelievably short time Jordan Sumner had had more impact on her than any man she had known for very much longer. That offhand invitation had delighted her, she had taken it to mean that he wanted to take their relationship a stage further, but to Jordan it seemed to have meant little, if anything at all. In which case, why had he ever bothered to ask her?

Frowning slightly, Madeleine recalled the withdrawal and carefully controlled restraint she had sensed in Jordan in the moments he had held her, the tension that had communicated a wish to be anywhere other than where he was. Could it be that he found her positively unattractive? But that didn't fit with the easy friend-liness he had shown all afternoon.

Lord, what was happening to her? She had never worried like this over other men's lack of interest; in fact, after Peter's unwelcome pushiness, Jordan's re-straint should make a pleasant change. Couldn't she just accept that she found him more attractive than he thought her, and leave it at that? Even as she asked herself the question, Madeleine knew that that would not satisfy her; she wanted, needed more.

'I think I shall have to go.' Jordan's voice broke in on her thoughts. 'The Evensleighs will have search parties out if I don't turn up soon. I only said I was going out for the day.'

Was that reluctance that threaded his voice? Stop it! Madeleine brought her thoughts under control with a struggle. Jordan wasn't some specimen to be dissected and examined minutely under a microscope, every word he said analysed to see if it had some hidden meaning. He had spent the whole day with her without any evi-dence of a wish to leave—surely that should tell her that he didn't positively *dislike* her!

'I'll drive you back,' she offered, getting to her feet.

'I don't want to impose on you—I'll get a taxi.'

'Jordan, this is rural Lincolnshire. The nearest all-night taxi firm is miles away. I can drive to the Manor and back in the time it would take them to get here.'

Driving down a darkened country lane, with the moon shining through the trees, casting unearthly, shifting shadows on the road in front of her, was an eerie ex-perience at the best of times, but tonight Madeleine seemed especially sensitive to the atmosphere. Her skin tingled with awareness, her pulses leaping with every faint movement from the silent man at her side, Jordan's shape just a darker, more substantial blur among the shadows. His eyes were fixed on the road ahead and his very stillness made her wonder if, in his mind's eye, he saw something other than the monotonous stretch of the white lines in the car's headlights.

Her own thoughts drifted back over the day, recalling the variable, changing moods Jordan had shown; sometimes coming close to some sort of an understanding, at others totally withdrawn and distant from her or, when that other, darkly shadowed part of his nature showed through, dangerously hostile. What lay behind those changes of mood she couldn't begin to guess, and she felt that, in spite of the light-hearted questions and answers they had shared over the meal, they were still very far apart, with Jordan still as much a stranger to her as when they had first met.

The wind whistling through the partly opened window whipped a long strand of dark hair over her face, catching at the corner of her mouth, and as she lifted a hand to pull it free the snatch of conversation she had overheard between Geraldine and Rupert which she now knew referred to Jordan surfaced in her mind. Sukey, Geraldine had said. Perhaps this was the answer to Jordan's careful keeping his distance. If there was some other woman in his life...

Suddenly the need to know overcame all considerations of tact or concern as to whether the question was one of those that would send Jordan back behind the invisible barriers he had erected between them. She was dangerously close to becoming deeply involved with this man, and for her own peace of mind she had to know.

'Will Sukey be living at Northcote, too?'

The effect of the question on Jordan was dramatic. Madeleine had barely time to register his sudden stiffening as his head swung round to face her, before she gave a cry of alarm as the wheel was snatched from her grasp and pulled on hard, swinging the car roughly to the side of the road.

In a reflex action Madeleine slammed her foot down on the brake, and with a protesting screech of tyres they shuddered to a halt, jolting her violently in her seat.

'What the hell do you think you're playing at?' Madeleine's voice shook with fear and anger as she rounded on Jordan. 'You could have killed us!'

Jordan had released the wheel and was sitting hunched in his seat, his ominous tautness making Madeleine think uneasily of some predatory animal crouched, ready to spring.

'Not what am *I* playing at!' His voice was a menacing snarl in the darkness. 'What's *your* game, lady? Who are you? Some friend of Sukey's?'

'I—but——'

Madeleine's voice failed her completely. She had glimpsed the darker side of Jordan in flashes throughout the day, but now she was brought up hard against the fact that the submerged part of his character seemed to have taken over. She had a frightening vision of the strength of his hand as it had gripped hers the day before, and shivered convulsively at the thought that she was alone with him on a dark and deserted country road.

The practical part of her mind seemed to be unaffected by the paralysis that held the rest of her frozen and, acting automatically, she reached forward to switch off the engine, taking the few seconds needed for the movement to draw breath, pull herself together.

'I don't know any Sukey,' she managed shakily as she sat back in her seat, her mind racing frantically, struggling with a desire to get out of the car and run from this Jordan who had suddenly transformed into a threatening stranger. But he *was* a stranger, she reminded herself. Apart from a few, trivial facts, she knew nothing about him.

'Sure you don't!' Jordan's eyes flashed eerily silver in the moonlight. 'Don't give me that rubbish, lady! If you don't know any Sukey, how come you asked about her?'

'I don't know any Sukey!' Madeleine repeated more emphatically. It was the only thing she could think of to say. Her head swam sickeningly with reaction to the shock of his sudden, violent reaction. 'I——'

But he wasn't going to give her a chance to explain. 'What's the game, Madeleine?' Jordan's voice was low and menacing, his stillness, after that one terrifying movement, somehow more frightening than if he had actually rounded on her. She could sense the violence simmering just under the surface, just as she had seen it flash in his eyes when Peter had drawn attention to his disability at the antiques fair, and it sparked off an answering anger in her own mind.

'No game, damn you! I might just as well ask what you're——' She broke off as a savage expletive tore into her words, recoiling sharply as Jordan's fist landed on the dashboard. 'Don't you swear at me, buster! I didn't start this!'

'No?'

The single syllable rang sharply in the confined space of the car and Madeleine shuddered at the sound of it. How could she even have liked this man? But this wasn't the Jordan who had spent the afternoon with her; it was as if someone else had taken his place. If only she could see him, read his face, it might help her, but the darkness hid every trace of his expression from her.

'Jordan, listen——' She had to get back in control, explain things calmly, but once again Jordan did not give her a chance to finish.

'No, you listen! I don't know what the hell's going on, I only know that you've spent all today asking questions, finding out all you can about me——'

Madeleine shrank back as Jordan flung up his hands in a gesture of angry frustration.

'I thought that this was far enough away from her— I thought I could find some peace here—but it was just my luck to run into someone who knew the little bitch!'

With a movement like that of a striking snake, Jordan reached out and gripped Madeleine's wrist with a bruising strength. Elsie's 'touch of steel' flashed into her thoughts with a new and terrifying intensity, only to be driven away completely by Jordan's next words.

'Did she put you up to this? How did she know I was here?'

'I don't know what you're talking about!' Madeleine's voice, high-pitched with tension, sounded strange and quite unlike itself. 'Jordan, you're hurting me!' The words were choked off on a sob of pain.

It froze him. Suddenly motionless and silent, he stared down at his powerful fingers, still clamped around her wrist, as if only now becoming aware of what he had done. In the taut silence Madeleine heard her own breathing, ragged and uneven, sounding abnormally loud in the quiet night.

'Christ!' The word hissed through Jordan's clenched teeth as he released her abruptly and lifted his hand to his own head, pressing his fingers hard against his temples as if to ease some intolerable ache.

'Jordan.' Madeleine tried to keep her voice calm and firm. 'Listen to me. I don't know any Sukey—I don't know anything about her.'

She saw his head come up, saw him turn to her, but the blackness was so intense that she couldn't penetrate it to read his expression.

'When you talk like that I could almost believe you,' he said slowly.

'You have to believe me—I'm telling the truth.'

'Then how did you know Sukey's name?' The question stabbed at her from the darkness.

'I—overheard someone——' She was strangely reluctant to reveal exactly who she had overheard, the memory of Geraldine's malicious laughter echoing in her thoughts.

'You'll have to do better than that,' Jordan came back at her inexorably.

'I can't.' It was just a whisper. If she said any more she would have to reveal exactly why it was so important to her to know if there was some other woman in his life, and she wasn't ready to put that into words just yet. In fact, she was no longer sure if she still felt that way. Those feelings had been for the other Jordan, not this frighteningly angry stranger.

'Then there's nothing more to say, is there?' With an abrupt movement Jordan freed his seat-belt and turned towards the door.

'Jordan—please——'

His hand on the doorhandle, he half turned back to her.

'Well?'

But it was impossible. She didn't even know where to begin. There *was* nothing more to say if he didn't believe the simple truth. Silently Madeleine shook her head, closing her eyes against the despair that tore through her, at the loss of the empathy they had shared earlier that day. She heard Jordan's savage curse, heard the door swing open violently and felt the rush of cold air as he swung himself out of the car. The slam of the door brought her eyes open in a rush.

'Jordan!'

But he hadn't—or wouldn't—hear her, and, knowing that there was no way she could reach him now, she could only sit and watch him walk away from her, his injured leg dragging roughly, until the darkness and her own tears blurred his retreating figure and he disappeared from sight.

'Northcote seems right for you—you look as if you belong here.' Her own words, spoken earlier, in the happier part of the day, came back to haunt her now. When she had said those words she had meant them and had felt a rush of happiness at the thought of Jordan living so close. But that was before the other, darker side of his personality had come so completely into the open. Now she no longer knew what she thought or felt about him, and the prospect of his coming to live at Northcote hung over her mind like a dark cloud, ominous and foreboding.

CHAPTER SIX

'WHAT the hell have you done to Jordan?' Peter's question brought Madeleine up short, the Staffordshire figure she had picked up to dust jolting precariously in her hand so that she had to set it down carefully before she could bring herself to answer.

'I haven't done anything to him!' she said sharply. 'What on earth are you talking about, Peter?'

It was five days since the visit to Northcote, five days in which she had neither seen Jordan nor heard from him. It was as if he had disappeared from her life as suddenly and mysteriously as he had come into it. But from the moment Peter had sauntered into the shop, full of self-confidence and clearly expecting her to be delighted to see him, she had known that it would not be long before the subject of his guest at the Manor would be raised. But she hadn't expected it in quite this way.

The image of Jordan's dark, angry figure moving slowly away from her floated before her eyes, and she closed them briefly to drive it away, only succeeding in reinforcing the picture and making it stand out more clearly.

'I haven't seen Mr Sumner since——' Madeleine broke off in confusion. How much did Peter know?

'Since you took him to Northcote—I know,' Peter said, answering one question at least. 'But you must have made quite an impression on him. He's been asking questions about you ever since.'

'Oh?' A wave of colour washed Madeleine's cheeks, betraying her disturbed reaction to that remark. 'What sort of questions?'

'Where you went to university; who you knew there; if you'd ever worked anywhere else—that sort of thing. Some I could answer, some I couldn't. After all, how should I know who your friends were at Nottingham? You'd already left when I met you. So I told him that if he wanted to know any more he'd better ask you himself.'

Madeleine made an inarticulate sound that might have been agreement. The flattered delight she had felt when Peter had said that Jordan had asked about her, the hope that that inexplicable argument had not destroyed things between them after all, fading before a worried uncertainty. These weren't the sort of questions someone asked about a friend they were interested in; they sounded more like an investigation into her background, and she didn't like that one little bit.

For a second she considered asking a few questions of her own, questions such as just who was Sukey and why did Jordan react so violently to her name? But then she dismissed the idea, feeling intuitively that, even if Peter knew the answer to them, Jordan would hate the idea that she had asked him. Irrational though it might be after the way he had treated her, she still felt that it was with Jordan that her loyalty lay.

'How is Jordan?' she forced herself to ask, picking up the duster and plying it with unnecessary vigour over an elegant sideboard.

Peter shrugged indifferently. 'So-so. Jordy's not the easiest of people to get on with at the best of times, and he was like a bear with a sore head at the beginning of the week. There was even some talk about him not buying the Hall after all, but packing his bags and clearing out.'

'But I thought it was all decided!' Madeleine heard the shock that sounded in her voice in spite of her efforts to conceal it. She had felt that Northcote was exactly what Jordan had been looking for and he had told her himself that he intended to buy it—so what had made him change his mind? And how would she feel about it if he didn't live at the Hall, after all? She found that she couldn't answer her own question.

'Well, it is now,' Peter said, oblivious to her ill-disguised confusion. 'We all went to the auction on Wednesday, and Jordan bought the place lock, stock and barrel. He's over at the solicitor's now, signing papers and lord-knows-what. That's why I'm here, I drove him into town.'

With care, Madeleine managed to stop her mouth from twisting into a wry grimace at the thought of how Jordan must have felt about that. If she was any judge, he must have hated being beholden to Peter in any way.

'Will that take long?'

It was an automatic question, used merely to keep the conversation from dying on its feet. The thought of Jordan being so close—the solicitor's office was only just across the street—was distinctly disturbing to her peace of mind. After the way they had parted on Sunday night, she was none too happy at the prospect of a meeting with him. At the sale of the contents of Northcote earlier that week, she had had trouble in concentrating on bidding for the items she wanted, her eyes constantly searching the crowded room to see if Jordan had attended the auction, too. It was only when she was quite sure that his still, erect figure was not among the crowd of prospective buyers that she had been able to settle down and concentrate on her task.

'About an hour. I suggested that he meet me here afterwards, before we go to the station.'

'Why the station?' It was an effort to ask the question naturally because of the nervous twisting of her stomach at the prospect of Jordan's imminent arrival in the shop.

'He has to book his seat on the train to London.' Seeing Madeleine's look of surprise, Peter elucidated further. 'He still has to see the specialist for a check-up once a month.'

'I see.'

It was impossible not to recall Jordan's cynically emphasised, 'I'm told I'll be able to *drive* very soon,' and his sharp-voiced response when she had foolishly asked about his riding. In the privacy of her own thoughts, Madeleine prayed that Jordan's doctor would have some good news for him this time.

'Is he planning on coming back?'

'For a week or so.' Peter sounded impatient, clearly none too pleased at the way the subject of Jordan was monopolising the conversation. 'Then he'll be off to Badminton on the fourteenth.'

'Badminton?' Madeleine could not disguise her astonishment at the news that Jordan was to attend the international three-day event. 'But surely Jordan——'

'Oh, he's not riding,' Peter broke in. 'How could he, with that leg of his?' Once more his tone grated on Madeleine's nerves, reminding her of the antipathy she had sensed between Jordan and Peter before. 'No, his brother's entered this year on one of the horses Jordan was training before the accident. Jordy's going along as back-up team and moral support. But, look, Maddy,'

Peter had tired of the subject of Jordan Sumner, 'I haven't even mentioned the reason I called——'

There was no need to, Madeleine thought wryly. She could guess only too easily.

'The Ball? Peter, I——' She broke off abruptly. She had been about to say, 'I'm going with Jordan,' but was that really true any longer? In the five days since the trip to Northcote, Jordan had made no effort to contact her either to confirm his invitation or withdraw it, and she wasn't exactly hard to find. Her home phone number and that of the shop were both in the directory, and Jordan knew where she lived. For a second she was strongly tempted to accept Peter's offer and fling Jordan Sumner's invitation in his face when he arrived in the shop.

That thought had her casting an uneasy glance out of the window in the direction of the solicitor's office, the knots in her stomach tightening unpleasantly as she saw the door swing open. But the figure that emerged was not Jordan and she relaxed again slightly, turning her attention back to the puzzle of the invitation to the Ball. The more realistic part of her brain told her that five days was quite long enough to wait for anyone, but another, more emotional part would keep reminding her of the moment Jordan's arms had come round her to comfort her.

'Come on, Maddy, say you'll come,' Peter urged. 'We'll have a great time—in fact, we'll have a Ball!'

Madeleine winced at the pun. 'I'm not sure, Peter. I— I have a friend who's coming to visit,' she improvised hastily and now, from dreading the moment of Jordan's arrival, she found she had changed to wishing he would appear. One look at his face would tell her whether she was foolish to hope that his outburst had been forgotten and that he wanted to revive the friendship there had been between them. 'I think she might be coming that weekend. Can you leave it with me and I'll check? The Ball's not till the twenty-sixth, is it? I'll let you know in good time, I promise.'

And that was a mistake, she admitted as soon as the words had left her mouth. Peter needed only the very slightest encouragement to become a positive nuisance. The fact that she had left the possibility of her agreeing to partner him open like that would very soon become, in his mind at least, a definite positive answer. If Jordan was to renew his invitation, she was going to find it very hard to extricate herself from what Peter would consider a firm agreement.

If Jordan wanted to renew the invitation, she repeated to herself with painful realism. Remembering the coldly savage anger that had filled him on Sunday night, Madeleine was forced to acknowledge that she would probably never have to face that particular problem.

'Has Jordan any plans to go back to Buckinghamshire?' she asked, unable to keep her mind off the subject of Jordan, in spite of Peter's evident disapproval.

'Not in the foreseeable future.'

Unexpectedly the answer came from the doorway, making her start in surprise before she swung round, her blue eyes wide and startled, meeting Jordan's smoky-grey ones as he moved into the shop. How had he come up on her without her noticing? She had only taken her eyes off the street for a few seconds. And how much of the conversation had he overheard? Had he listened to her fumbling attempt to put Peter off and, if so, what interpretation would he put on it? But the cold light in Jordan's eyes told her only one thing—that he had caught the question he had answered and, remembering his angry comment about her asking questions before, she felt a sensation like the trickle of cold water run down her spine. One taste of that other, darker side of him had been enough, she had no wish to repeat the experience. She shifted uneasily from one foot to another under the intensity of his gaze, uneasily aware of the fact that her surprised start could well have been taken as a gesture of guilt at being caught prying if one was in that frame of mind which, to judge from the swift narrowing of his eyes, was just the sort of mood Jordan was in.

'Everything signed and sealed then, Jordy?' Peter put in, oblivious to the atmosphere that had suddenly descended, seeming to thicken around Madeleine with every second that passed so that she found it difficult to breathe naturally, a fact which clearly hadn't escaped those probing silver eyes.

A curt nod was Jordan's only response; his attention was centred firmly on Madeleine's face, his own expression cold and hard as stone.

'But I shall have to go back to arrange for the transportation of the horses,' he continued, as if Peter hadn't spoken. 'Though that will only take a day or so.'

Of course, the horses. Madeleine thought back, recalling how he had said that Northcote was a place where his horses could be comfortable. Always, it seemed, those animals came first, before any other consideration.

Now that the shock of Jordan's sudden appearance had eased slightly, she found herself able to look at him clearly for the first time, taking in the way the navy sweater he wore clung to the muscular lines of his shoulders and chest, the harsh denim of his jeans outlining the strength of his legs and thighs in a way that made her heart seem to turn over inside her. When he stood next to Peter like this the difference in their heights

was evident, and yet Jordan was in no way over-
shadowed by the other man's extra inches. In some
strange way Peter's glowing handsomeness seemed to
fade into insignificance, as if he had become just a
painted cardboard cut-out, so that all she was aware of
was the trained power of Jordan's body, the stunning
impact of those light-coloured eyes. Madeleine hadn't
noticed that she had become so absorbed until Jordan's
sudden movement as he lifted his hand jolted her back
to reality.

'I brought these for you.'

For a long, stunned moment Madeleine simply stared
at the bouquet of flowers he held out, unable to take in
what he had said, but a second later her thoughts cleared
and she felt her heart lift in a soaring sensation of delight. He had brought her flowers! The quarrel of Sunday
night was to be forgotten.

Not caring if what she was feeling showed openly in
her face, she lifted glowing eyes to look Jordan straight
in the face, but what she saw there and his next words
brought her back down to earth with a bump.

'They're my way of saying thank you for taking me
to Northcote.'

Thank you—and goodbye. He didn't have to say it,
it was written all over his face, and Madeleine felt her
short-lived joy tumbling around her, to lie in ruins at
her feet as the truth hit home.

What about dinner—what about the Ball? she wanted
to cry but choked the words back with a painful effort.
There would be no dinner, the invitation to the Ball was
well and truly forgotten, that was obvious. The cold formality of Jordan's tone and expression made everything
so sharply clear that it stabbed like the point of a razor-
sharp knife. She had taken him to Northcote, he was

thanking her with flowers—and that was an end to it. It was as if the time they had spent together after the trip to the Hall had never been.

'They're—they're lovely.'

Her tongue felt thick and clumsy, stumbling over the words as she took the flowers from Jordan. He stepped back as soon as she had them, she noted miserably, putting a physical distance between them as well as the mental one that was now all too evident.

'Thank you very much.' She was unable to control the way her voice shook on the murmured words.

'I appreciated what you did.'

Had that low-toned voice ever warmed with friend-liness and amusement? Madeleine found herself won-dering. It was now so cool and clipped that she could almost believe she had dreamed the difference in it on Sunday.

'It was nothing—you didn't need to——' She framed the words automatically, lowering her eyes to the flowers so that she did not have to look into his face. But the image of it still floated in her mind, hard and set, his eyes just grey chips of ice, and she felt her blood chill as if his gaze had had an actual, physical effect.

'I like to say thank you properly.'

The stiff precision of those words had her tightening her hand around the flowers, crushing the delicate stems as she fought an impulse to fling the bouquet in his face, to declare that she didn't want this thanks, she wanted—what? What did she want? Madeleine asked herself un-happily. Things to be as they had been? But what there had been between them was only the tentative rapport of two people who had just met and who found each other pleasant company, nothing more. All those other feelings, that strange sense of familiarity, the closeness, the comfort she had drawn from him, had all been just creations of her own fantasy. She had wanted it to be so, and because of that had imagined there to be more than there was—or had she?

Unable to stop herself, Madeleine cast a swift glance at Jordan's face, hoping to see something that might help her there. But Jordan had already turned to Peter.

'I think it's time we were heading for the station.'

And that was that. Madeleine managed a stilted goodbye, received an equally stiff one in reply, and the two men departed, leaving her standing in the centre of the shop, Jordan's flowers still in her hands. It was only when the two figures turned the corner at the end of the road and disappeared from sight that she looked down at the bouquet, a dreary, nagging ache starting up inside her as she surveyed its bright, glowing colours, a gaiety totally at odds with the way she was feeling.

She had hoped for time, for the chance to get to know Jordan better, to understand him, but that time had been denied her. With a low cry she flung the bouquet from her, heedless of the way it landed awkwardly on a nearby table, damaging some of the delicate blooms. It's over, she told herself, over and done with. We were just ships that passed in the night, nothing more, forget him. *Forget him,* she repeated more emphatically, but even as she did so the words sounded hollow and meaningless. In such a short time Jordan had got through to her in a way she'd never anticipated. She doubted if she would ever be able to forget him; in fact, she rather suspected that she didn't even want to.

In the days that followed, that suspicion lingered in Madeleine's mind, making her abstracted by day and restless, unable to sleep, by night. She couldn't get Jordan out of her thoughts, couldn't stop wondering how his visit to the specialist had gone, whether he had moved into Northcote yet, but she was unable to discover any clear facts about him until she met up with Geraldine Fry at the local hairdressers' where Madeleine had gone for her regular six-weekly trim.

Absorbed in the inevitable struggle with the stylist, who was determined to persuade her into a more adventurous style, Madeleine didn't notice the occupant of the chair next to her until, in a brief pause when Zena had disappeared to advise on a perm for another customer, she heard Geraldine's plummy tones.

'Hairdressers can be so domineering, can't they? I hope I'm not going to have all that bother when it's my turn. I don't often come in here, of course—I usually go to my regular stylist in Nottingham—but Rupe's taking me out tonight, and I just can't manage to put my hair up on my own.' She smoothed the gleaming blonde mane as she spoke. 'Are you sticking to your guns, then? Nothing new?'

'No.' Madeleine shook her head, sending the damp strands of her newly washed hair flying. Geraldine stretched exaggeratedly as if easing tense muscles.

'God, am I glad to get away from the Manor! Jordan was in an absolute swine of a mood, snapping and snarling at everyone like a bad-tempered terrier.'

'He's back, then?' Inane as it sounded, it was all Madeleine could manage. In spite of her resolution that the best, the only thing she could do was to forget Jordan once and for all, she had still found herself listening for the sound of the telephone, her heart lurching when it rang, only to sink right down again when she heard some other voice at the other end of the line.

'Oh, yes, he got back on Thursday night—and personally I shall be quite pleased when he takes himself off to Badminton. Just because the doctor wasn't too happy with his progress doesn't give him the right to take it out on his friends.'

Madeleine flinched inside at the careless words. Didn't Geraldine understand how much it meant to Jordan to be able to ride again? And, remembering Geraldine's catty tone when she had talked of Jordan and Sukey, she felt like questioning the other woman's use of the word 'friends'.

'Have you known Jordan long?'

'A couple of years.' Geraldine's attention was on her hands, a frown creasing her forehead at the sight of some tiny flaw in the vivid varnish. 'Of course, Rupe's known him much longer. His mother and Jordan's were at school together and the boys met up quite often when they both started riding competitively.'

'Peter said something about Jordan winning the World Championships.'

'Lord, yes!' Geraldine turned wide blue eyes on Madeleine, as if astounded by her ignorance. 'He won the Individual Gold three years running. You name it, Jordan's won it—European, World, and of course the Olympic Gold. He was all set to be in this year's Olympic team too, but of course that's not on the cards any more. With that leg of his, and his best horse dead, he'll be well out of competitions for some time yet.'

'His horse died?' Madeleine's shock showed in her voice.

'Broke a leg—had to be shot.' Geraldine's tone was matter-of-fact. 'Damn shame, really. He had this black mare—Swallow—she was one of the most brilliant cross-country horses I've ever seen.'

Swallow. In her mind Madeleine heard again Rupert's careless, 'He can't still be brooding over Swallow.' She hadn't understood the name at the time, but she did now.

'What happened?' Her voice croaked on the question. Well aware of Jordan's concern for his horses, she could easily imagine just what Swallow's death had meant to him.

'No one's really sure. Jordan was schooling the mare, putting her over some practice jumps about a mile from the house, and it was only when he didn't come back that Michael went to look for him. All I know is that the horse had fallen and Jordan was trapped underneath her. He was unconscious when they found him, and he's never fully explained what happened—I don't suppose he remembers much of it. Rupe says he must have put Swallow at the jump all wrong, she wasn't the sort of animal to be thrown by some piddling little practice fence. Jordan took it very badly when he learned she'd been put down. I suppose he blamed himself for the accident.'

Zena had returned, brandishing her scissors, and an assistant came to take Geraldine through to have her hair washed, but Madeleine scarcely saw her go, nor did she hear Zena's careless chatter about the weather and her latest boyfriend. Her mind was full of thoughts of Jordan and the accident Geraldine had described so off-handedly. She could well imagine what the loss of Swallow had meant to Jordan; the times he had talked about his horses and riding had been the only occasions on which emotion had crept into that carefully controlled voice, except for the anger that had erupted on the journey back to the Manor, when she had asked him about Sukey.

Sukey and Swallow—the two names seemed somehow linked, caught up in the story of Jordan's accident. But there was no way she would ever find out exactly what had happened. She doubted if she would ever see Jordan again and, if she did, his attitude at their last meeting had made it very clear that he would never let her get close enough to ask him.

'Peter phoned,' her mother announced as she walked into the house. 'You didn't tell me you were going to the Ball with him.'

I didn't tell Peter I was, either, Madeleine was tempted to retort, but she bit back the words. Jordan had been back at the Manor for two days now; he hadn't phoned or called round at the shop in that time. How much longer was she going to pretend that there was any chance of him being her partner?

'What are you going to wear?' Lucina asked. 'You'll need something a bit special. It'll be a very posh do by all accounts, very formal. It's a wonderful excuse to buy something new.'

But I'm not going! With an effort Madeleine caught the words before she spoke them. Jordan had cut himself off from her, but Peter was making it all too plain how much he wanted her as his partner, and she wouldn't be human if she didn't admit to a secret longing to attend one of the exclusive social gatherings that were the talk of the neighbourhood. For just once in her life she would love to go to a proper ball with a beautiful dress to wear and a handsome, dinner-jacketed escort at her side— and Peter was only too willing to provide the latter.

Or should she wait, give Jordan one more chance? No. Madeleine's lips firmed and she shook off the weak thought, admitting it was pure self-deception. Jordan had already had a second chance—and a third, if it came to that.

'How about a trip to Lincoln next week, Mum?' she asked impulsively. 'Wednesday's half-closing day, we could shut up a bit early and have lunch out before spending the afternoon shopping.'

'That sounds like fun.' Lucina's turquoise eyes sparkled in anticipation.

'Then it's settled—and you can help me choose a dress.'

'For the Ball?'

'For the Ball,' Madeleine agreed firmly. 'I want something really special, something that will make me look glamorous and sexy.'

'I know just the shop. And you mustn't worry about the cost—I'll buy it for you as an early birthday present. You'll be the belle of the Ball. We'll find something that'll knock Peter Evensleigh for six!'

Well, perhaps it would, Madeleine thought drily, but Peter wasn't the man she planned on affecting in that way. She had no idea whether Jordan Sumner would attend the Ball, since he had made it so plain that he didn't want her as his partner any more, but *she* was going—and if Jordan should happen to be there then she'd make very sure that he knew exactly what he was missing!

CHAPTER SEVEN

MADELEINE'S mirror told her that she'd got the effect she wanted, and her mother's enthusiasm reinforced that conviction, but if she had needed any further proof then Peter's reaction left her in no doubt that she looked better than she had ever done in her life. His jaw practically hit the floor when she opened the door to him on the night of the Ball.

'God, Madeleine!' he gasped, his blue eyes wide.

'Like it?' Madeleine spun round, her eyes sparkling.

From the moment she had seen the dress, she had known it was right. In kingfisher-blue silk satin, it was a 'nothing' of a dress, the simplest of shifts with long sleeves and a V-neckline; the sort of dress that looked limp and shapeless on a hanger, but when put on it clung lovingly to the lines of her body, emphasising and enhancing every curve in a way that was more subtly sensual than any more blatantly revealing dress.

With Zena's help she had created a new, more sophisticated style for her hair, catching it up in two separate ponytails, one on the top of her head and a second further down on the right-hand side, sweeping the thick dark mane up to fall in a cascading tumble of shining curls. Subtle use of make-up emphasised her cheekbones and eyes, the shade of her dress and a touch of sparkling blue eyeshadow picking up and deepening their colour so that for the first time she saw that they were not nondescript but a clear, glowing blue. A tiny evening bag and dainty sandals completed the outfit. She wore no jewellery, for the dress needed no adornment, and she let it speak for itself.

'Maddy, you look stunning!'

Peter did indeed, as her mother had predicted, look knocked for six, and his open admiration eased the nagging ache that had filled her as she'd dressed, unable to stop her thoughts from straying on to the subject of how different it might have been if she had been going to the ball with Jordan, after all. So she found it easy to forget her earlier reservations about having him as her escort as she smiled up into his admiring blue eyes. She even found it possible to forgive him his persistent shortening of her name.

Perhaps Peter wasn't the man she would have chosen as a partner, but all the same he was an undeniably attractive male, his tall frame enhanced by the black evening suit he wore, its colour reflecting the dark sheen of his hair and throwing into sharper definition those blue, blue eyes. If the front of his immaculate white shirt was a little too frilled for her personal liking, and the scent of his aftershave so potent it overwhelmed her own perfume, well, those were only small points, and she refused to let herself think of Jordan's compact strength and withdrawn, austere face as she followed Peter out to the car.

'Will there be many people there tonight?' she asked as the sleek red sports car leapt forward and Peter grinned his response.

'Hundreds. I think Ma's invited the entire county—not to mention the friends who have come up from London. We've had a house full since Friday.'

That must take some doing, Madeleine reflected, recalling the Manor's fifteen bedrooms. Beside it, even

Northcote Hall looked small. Mentally she jumped, she mustn't start thinking of Jordan——

'And you have a guest already.'

How had that happened? She had only just determined *not* to mention Jordan, and immediately a comment that led indirectly to his name had slipped out.

'Jordy, you mean? Oh, he's not with us any more. He moved into Northcote to supervise the alterations when he got back from Badminton.'

'I didn't know that.'

But now that she did, how did it make her feel? She didn't need any confirmation of the fact that Jordan no longer had a place for her in his life, but the thought that he hadn't bothered to tell her of his move twisted something deep inside her, so that she moved restlessly in her seat.

'Will he be coming tonight?' she asked and found Peter's shrug of uncertainty both a relief and a disappointment.

'I dunno. He's invited, of course, but there's not a lot of point in coming to a ball if you can't dance, is there?'

That was true, but she didn't like the mocking tone in which Peter had uttered that last remark—though why she should feel so defensive about a man who had treated her so badly was quite beyond her.

Suddenly deflated, Madeleine stared out at the darkened countryside, admitting to herself that she had been keyed-up for this evening, that all her care, all her preparations, had been based on the belief that Jordan would be at the Ball to see her—and now that that fact was in doubt she suffered a severe pang of conscience at the thought that she was just using Peter in order to get her revenge for the slight she felt Jordan had inflicted on her.

No, not *using*, she told herself firmly. Peter had wanted her to be his partner tonight and she had agreed to that, nothing more. She had never made any secret of the fact that there couldn't be any real relationship between them, and on those terms she was being perfectly fair. She would put Jordan firmly out of her thoughts, she resolved, and concentrate on enjoying herself in Peter's company. She could still have a very pleasant evening that way.

By ten o'clock her resolution was wavering and her smile was becoming more fixed and false with every minute that passed. From the moment of their arrival at the Manor, Madeleine and Peter had been swept into the close-knit group that formed the Evensleigh set, central to which were Rupert and Geraldine, the latter now proudly sporting a huge diamond on the third finger of her left hand which she took every opportunity of waving under the nose of anyone who didn't know about her engagement. Madeleine had danced several times with Peter and once with Rupert and a couple of other male members of the party, but now the majority of the group seemed content to lounge in their chairs, downing champagne and chatting desultorily.

The conversation centred on Rupert and Geraldine's plans for an August wedding, in which Madeleine was able to assume an interest. The usual hunting, shooting and fishing topics left her completely cold. Only when the talk veered on to the subject of the recent Badminton Horse Trials did she discover a spark of interest.

But even then she was disappointed. The technical details of dressage and cross-country speed and endurance tests were like a foreign language to her and, as no one bothered to explain, all she learned was that Michael Sumner had acquitted himself creditably, coming twelfth out of seventy-four competitors. When Jordan's name was mentioned, it was only in connection with his past victories or as the owner and, originally, trainer of the horse his brother had ridden. That was not the sort of information Madeleine wanted to know, and it only added to her burning sense of frustration and disappointment.

Disconsolately she surveyed the crowded ballroom, toying listlessly with her glass as she considered the jewel-bright colours of the women's dresses in glowing contrast to the severe black and white of the men's clothes, the pounding music making her temples throb painfully.

What was she doing here? Jordan wasn't coming, she had long since given up searching the crowd for his slim, erect figure, and without the spark of excitement that the idea of showing him how little she cared for his neglect had brought, the evening seemed flat and dull. Peter had embarked on a long and involved joke concerning an Irishman, a penguin and a five-pound note, and the few hours between now and midnight when she could consider going home stretched ahead like a barren eternity.

She needed some air. The weather was unseasonably mild and the heavy, smoky atmosphere was overpowering. With a murmured explanation to Peter who, caught up in his story, barely saw her go, she moved away, heading for the doors that led out on to the terrace.

Pausing in the doorway to gulp down long, refreshing breaths of the night air, Madeleine suddenly froze as, out of the corner of her eye she caught a faint movement from a shadowy figure that set her nerves quivering, making her tremble in response. She didn't need to turn her head to discover the source of the prickling awareness; she could feel Jordan's still, silent presence with every instinct she possessed. In the space of a second, she half turned to retreat back into the ballroom, then corrected the movement to take several determined steps out on to the terrace. She wasn't going to be frightened into flight, though the cold pins and needles that filled her veins made her legs unsteady beneath her.

'Good evening, Miss Crawford.' Jordan's voice came to her on the still night air.

He was leaning against the wall at the far end of the terrace, a glass in one hand, his face completely in shadow, and only the immaculate white of his shirt showing clearly in the darkness.

'Mr Sumner.' Madeleine made her acknowledgement equally formal, the tightness of her voice putting an almost tangible distance between them.

But it wasn't just her feelings of uncertainty that kept her head stiffly erect and froze the carefully polite smile on her face; there was also the shock of discovering that he was here, after all, and had been—for how long? All her ideas of showing him how little she cared for his rejection fled suddenly, as she admitted to herself how much she had wanted to see him—and not just for the reasons she had originally allowed herself to believe.

'I didn't know you were here.' She spoke without thinking, the hurt echoing unconsciously in her voice.

'Oh, I haven't been here long.' Jordan straightened up slowly. 'This sort of do isn't really my thing, but I felt obliged to put in an appearance for courtesy's sake.'

'Really?' Madeleine wished she could bring her voice down a degree or two. It sounded high-pitched and brittle, betraying her over-stretched nerves to any careful listener. She didn't want him to know how easily he could affect her simply by being there. 'I thought this *was* your usual social scene—balls in country houses——'

His stillness and the tiny but unbridgeable distance between them was getting to her and she fumbled for words.

'—riding with the hunt, that sort of thing.'

'You sound as if you disapprove.' Jordan's tone was mild and expressionless, in contrast to the steel-shuttered coldness that had filled it the last time they had met.

'I do!' Madeleine snatched at the opening he had given her to be honest. 'I think hunting's cruel and unnecessary.'

'As a matter of fact, so do I.'

The quiet answer took the ground from under her feet. She didn't want to be reminded of the closeness of mind they had shared that afternoon in her house, and her hard-won composure threatened to shatter as Jordan came to stand beside her, the soft, dragging sound of his movement scraping against her over-sensitive nerves so that she bit down hard on her lower lip. Perversely, having felt his distance from her so strongly at first, she now wanted him to be much further away.

Her earlier scheme of impressing Jordan with her appearance, of showing him just who he had rejected, now seemed foolish and over-optimistic. He hadn't even spared her a second glance, damn him, which was all the more disturbing when she was so intensely aware of the honed strength of his body beneath the beautifully tailored clothes that fitted like a second skin. No lacy ruffles softened the severity of his shirt, the only scent that reached her was the subtlest hint of some tangy cologne, mixed with the more potent aroma of his skin, and in the moonlight his austere face had a strong, unearthly beauty that set her senses quivering.

'Heard from Sukey lately?'

The unexpected question stabbed like an ice-cold knife, taking her unawares so that she drew in her breath in shock, gasping like a small, frightened animal suddenly discovering that it was cornered. With an effort she pulled herself back under control.

'I've told you I don't know any Sukey, Mr Sumner.'

It had taken perhaps three seconds for her to recover, turn and direct a coolly confident face towards him, but as she met his eyes and saw them gleaming coldly silver in the light of the moon she knew that that momentary hesitation had been fatal. Jordan lifted one eyebrow in sardonic disbelief.

'I know what you told me.' The soft words were tinged with a thread of menace. 'But you'll have to forgive me if I choose to believe otherwise.'

His hostility was almost tangible, beating at her thoughts like waves pounding against cliffs, so that it was a struggle to think clearly. Madeleine had opened her lips to shoot back an angry retort but, reconsidering, she closed them firmly against it, swallowing hard to relieve the dryness in her throat.

She had every right to feel annoyance at his sceptical dismissal of her words, but along with her anger she was experiencing a whole new set of feelings, painful sensations of loss and unhappiness brought on by his cold antagonism. If she didn't clamp down on the volatile mixture, the result could be a devastatingly destructive explosion. She had to be calm.

'You can believe what you want,' she said quietly.' *I* know I'm telling the truth, and that's all that matters.'

That struck home. She could almost feel the reverberations caused by her words, rippling through the air like the waves created when a stone is thrown into a pond. Jordan's head went back in shock, bringing his face directly into the light for the first time, and Madeleine's heart twisted at the sight of it.

The eerie gleam of the moon had drained all colour from his skin, casting frightening shadows around his eyes so that they were just dark, impenetrable pools, no gleam of life or feeling in their sombre depths. The muscles in his jaw were pulled tight, stretching his skin harshly over the hard bones of his face.

'Do you expect me to accept that?' he asked harshly, and Madeleine struggled with a longing to reach out and grasp his arms, shake the truth into him by force, if necessary.

But such an action would be fatal. She knew intuitively that Jordan would reject it violently, and she also knew that she would not be able to bear it if he did. Tension stretched her nerves so tightly that she felt as if a steel band was drawn tight around her head, digging deeper into her skin with every second that passed. Nervously, she wetted painfully dry lips with her tongue, and saw the flash of silver as his eyes followed the tiny movement.

'You can accept it or reject it, as you please.' To her relief, her voice revealed nothing of her internal conflict, but was as calm and even as she could wish. 'I'm not a liar, Mr Sumner, and I object to being thought one on such fragile evidence. In fact, I find it positively insulting!'

Jordan's breath hissed between clenched teeth. 'Sukey knows I'm here,' he declared roughly.

'Well, bully for Sukey!' Madeleine's control snapped, making her lash out verbally, using the taut flippancy of her tone to disguise the bitter disappointment that clawed at her at his stubborn refusal to believe her. 'And I suppose you think I told her?'

'She had to find out from someone,' Jordan pointed out with icy reasonableness.

'Well, not from me!' Madeleine's voice echoed round the silent terrace.

With a tiny part of her mind she caught the sounds of the Ball from inside the house; music and talk and the shuffle of feet on the dance-floor, sounds she had been deaf to until now, as if they had faded away in the moment she had become aware of Jordan's presence.

Briefly she wondered where Peter was, if he was looking for her, or if, caught up in his role as joker and raconteur, he had even noticed she had gone. She knew a weak longing to turn, go back into that crowded ballroom, lose herself in the noise and the bustle, and break off from Jordan completely. But even as the thought crossed her mind she knew she could never do it. Jordan had got under her skin, making her feel that she really understood the phrase for the first time, and she couldn't break free from the inexplicable and indefinable hold he had over her.

'Who else is there?' Jordan flung the question at her.

'Rupert,' Madeleine flashed back. 'Geraldine—Peter—any one of a dozen people.'

'They've never even mentioned her name to me!' Jordan dismissed the suggestion with a gesture that matched the violence in his voice.

'And I have?'

'Yes!'

'And on that evidence you condemn me—guilty until proven innocent!' Bitterness rang in Madeleine's voice. It would be easy to explain, to tell him of the conversation she had overheard, but two things held her back. For a start, the mood Jordan was in she doubted if he would even listen to her and second, and perhaps more important, she wanted to be believed for herself, not because of evidence she could produce to contradict his assumption. 'For God's sake, Jordan, what is this woman to you?'

In the moment she rounded on him, she saw Jordan's eyes narrow until they were just slits in his face. Her heart lurched painfully, setting a nervous pulse racing through her body. How could she ever have thought of this man as a friend?

'Why do you hate Sukey, Jordan? What did she do to you?' The words spilled out automatically with the force of a fast-flowing torrent, she couldn't have held them back if she'd tried. Hot tears burned her eyes, blurring her vision so that she hadn't the strength to resist when, with a sudden movement, Jordan grasped her wrists, holding them in a painfully bruising grip.

'What did she tell you?' His voice was low and savage.

'Noth——' Her voice failed her, and it was only with a supreme effort that she was able to try again. '*Nothing!* Jordan—I don't know this Sukey or anything about her. Would—would I have asked those questions if I did? You have to believe me, I don't know anything!'

She choked on the last word, tension, fear and something close to despair destroying her defences, so that the tears she had fought against earlier spilled over and coursed down her cheeks, and there was nothing she could do to hold them back.

The effect on Jordan was electric. Shock, concern and suspicion followed each other across his face and, frighteningly, it was suspicion that held and set hard and unyielding. Without any need of words, Madeleine suddenly knew that tears had been Sukey's weapon, one used with devastating effect until something had brought about the final break.

'I'm sorry!' She tried to pull her hands free to brush the tears away, but Jordan's grip tightened and she was held transfixed in a moment that seemed frozen out of time like a film that had suddenly stopped.

'Maddy! Maddy, are you there?'

She heard Peter's voice, but couldn't turn to acknowledge his call, mesmerised by the burning intensity in Jordan's eyes.

'Maddy?' Footsteps sounded behind them.

'Oh, bloody hell, pretty-boy Evensleigh!'

The film shifted, moved on as Jordan dropped Madeleine's hands as if they burned him and, after one swift, searching glance at her face, moved slightly in Peter's direction, positioning himself so that his body blocked the other man's line of vision, hiding Madeleine from him.

'So this is where you've been hiding yourself.'

Madeleine sensed rather than saw Peter's double-take as he came on to the terrace and saw that she was not alone.

'Oh, hello, Jordy.'

'Good evening, Peter.'

Madeleine was stunned by the casual ease of Jordan's tone, the complete switch from the intense emotion of only seconds before. Belatedly she realised that Jordan's position was deliberate. He was shielding her from Peter, giving her a chance to pull herself together and compose her face into something like calm. In spite of all that had happened he was still showing her such consideration. Deeply grateful for those few moments' grace, she brushed at her damp face, trying to erase the signs of the emotional storm that had shaken her.

'What are you doing here?' Belligerence at finding Jordan with 'his' girl coloured Peter's tone, and with a bitter taste in her mouth Madeleine remembered Jordan's laughing declaration that he would love to see Peter's face if he saw them together.

'I was invited,' Jordan answered calmly, clearly deliberately misunderstanding the question.

'But we didn't think you were coming. How did you get here?'

'I drove.'

It was a quiet, matter-of-fact explanation, but it reached Madeleine. In her delight at this news of his progress she abandoned her attempts at repairs and turned a glowing face towards the two men.

'You *drove*! Oh, Jordan, that's wonderful!' She saw the change in Jordan's face, the wary light in his eyes as if he was uncertain how to react to her enthusiasm. 'And what about riding?'

The light died like a candle suddenly extinguished by the wind.

'Not yet,' Jordan said curtly.

'Maddy, it's time for supper. I came to find you to take you into the dining-room.' Absorbed in his own irritation, Peter was oblivious to the tension in the atmosphere. 'How long have you been out here?'

'Not long. I—I had a headache,' Madeleine improvised hastily, intensely grateful for the shadows on the terrace that hid the marks of tears on her face. When she went back inside she would have to make a quick dash to the bathroom to carry out some vital repairs to her appearance. 'I came out for some fresh air and met Jordan. I'm sorry, I didn't notice the time. We were— talking.'

'What about?' Peter sounded suspicious.

Jordan was still watching her, she could feel his eyes on her face. She had to be very careful what she said next. And then the phrase Jordan had used when they had been talking about her father slid into her mind and she seized on it thankfully, suddenly knowing exactly how to go on.

'About horses.'

'Really?' Peter's astonishment was clear. 'I thought you weren't interested in such things.'

'I'm learning.' Madeleine kept her eyes on Peter, but every nerve was alive to Jordan's watchful presence. 'For instance, I never knew just how important mucking-out could be.'

A tiny start from the man at her side told her that the dart had hit home, and a swift, sidelong glance at his face met those grey eyes, now dark and searching as if he wanted to probe beneath the surface of what she had said and read her true meaning. With a sudden rush of new confidence, she smiled gently into his troubled face.

'That's right, isn't it, Jordan?'

For a fraction of a second he hesitated, then very slowly he nodded.

'That's exactly right,' he said and a new, husky note in his voice caught at her heart, so that it was a struggle to keep her own tone even when she spoke again.

'Perhaps we can talk again some time. I'd like to learn a lot more about it.'

Peter was becoming impatient; she would have to leave it at that. Madeleine didn't look back as she let Peter take her arm and lead her into the ballroom, but she could feel Jordan's eyes on her as she moved away, his cloudy gaze burning into her spine until she crossed the threshold and was swallowed up in the crowd.

CHAPTER EIGHT

'WHAT the hell are you doing here with *him*?'

Madeleine had known that Jordan would seek her out again—he wasn't likely to leave things as unsatisfactorily incomplete as they were—but she hadn't expected it to be quite so soon, nor had she anticipated that he would launch straight into the attack—at least, not on this particular subject.

But the moment supper was over and Peter had left her, as he put it, to perform his filial duty and dance with his mother, Jordan had emerged from the crowd without warning, pouncing with the speed and stealth of a hunting tiger.

'Peter invited me to the Ball—you know that!'

It was a struggle to keep her tone calm, the temptation to retort that she was here with Peter because he, Jordan, had abandoned her without so much as a second thought almost overwhelming.

'I also know that you didn't want to be his partner,' Jordan snarled, his anger setting her nerves jangling so that her fingers sought the sleeve of her dress, twisting unconsciously in the soft material and crushing it irreparably. 'Damn it, Madeleine, you don't even *like* him!'

'I—I haven't been to a ball since I was at university.' Madeleine's tongue felt thick and clumsy, making her stumble over her words. Why should Jordan be so furiously angry at the way she had accepted Peter's invitation? It didn't make sense, not when he had made it so plain that he didn't want to partner her himself.

'And—and I'd just bought this dress, and I wanted an opportunity to wear it.'

She regretted the words as soon as they were spoken, because they drew Jordan's eyes to the blue dress, skimming over the feminine lines of her body in a glance that began as cold appraisal, but changed half-way into something very different, something that made her heart stop and then jerk back into action at an alarmingly increased pace.

When he lifted his eyes to hers once more, the world tilted and swung round her as she saw how dark they were, the pupils dilated until they were almost all black.

Dear God, he wasn't immune to her as she had thought. He wasn't even indifferent! And, after the distance, the coldness of his rigid control, she thought the fire of desire she could read in his gaze would shrivel her where she stood.

'You look very beautiful.' The unexpectedly warmly sensual note in his voice dried her throat.

'Th-thank you,' she croaked hoarsely, not knowing how to handle this very different Jordan. Two weeks ago she might have welcomed this, it would have been all she would have wanted to know, that the attraction she felt towards this man was reciprocated, but now it brought her no happiness at all. What good was passion without trust? Her heart ached as she acknowledged that desire was not enough, she wanted more. Her fingers tugged at her sleeve, pushing the rich blue satin back from her wrist.

'What's this?'

Without warning Jordan's hand had snaked out, fastening over the delicate bones, lifting and turning her wrist to the light. With a jolt of shock Madeleine saw what he had seen, the dark stains of bruises already forming, disfiguring the pale skin. Silently Jordan moved his own hand, adjusting the position of his strong fingers until they covered the marks exactly. For a long, taut moment he simply stared at the evidence of his own strength, then his eyes lifted and looked straight into Madeleine's blue ones.

'I hurt you,' he said huskily, and on her wrist his thumb moved softly, smoothing the damaged flesh in a gentle caress. 'I'm sorry.'

Madeleine wanted to snatch her hand away, but at the same time she desperately wanted to leave it where it was. That tiny, unconscious movement was setting the blood in her veins alight with liquid fire, the heat of which seemed to melt her bones. If he had been anyone but Jordan she would have put her other hand on his arm and moved forward, lifting her face for his kiss, but the memory of his sudden withdrawal the one time he had held her stilled the impulse. Jordan wouldn't accept her approaches, she knew; too much had been said for that, too much that had to be healed.

'Yes, you hurt me.' Her voice was soft. 'But I think you were hurting badly, too.'

The gentle movement of Jordan's thumb stopped abruptly, and his hand was snatched away, the coldness of his eyes forcefully rejecting her tentative approach. Madeleine's sense of loss was like a blow in her face, sending her thoughts reeling so that she almost cried aloud in pain.

'Jordan.' His name came out shakily. 'Jordan, we have to talk.'

'Do we?'

The two curt syllables were not encouraging, but she had to make herself go on, she had to have one last try to break down the barriers that had come between them, to try to restore the unity they had known so briefly. She had had no difficulty in talking to him then, but now her mind felt bruised and numb and it was difficult to think clearly.

'Yes, we do—I have to talk to you about—about—oh!'

She broke off on a startled yelp, her train of thought shattered as a warm, possessive arm slid round her waist from behind, drawing her back against a firm male chest.

'Hello, gorgeous. Missed me?'

Damn you, Peter! Blind, irrational fury filled Madeleine's mind so that she was tempted to jab an elbow backwards into Peter's stomach, forcing him to release her. The scent of his aftershave was cloying, sickening, and she tensed against that possessive hold, her eyes going to Jordan's face. But even as they did so she knew it was already too late—the fragile link she had tried to forge had snapped, the barriers were up again, Jordan's expression shuttered and remote. She could beat against those steel walls until her fists were bleeding, but to no avail.

'Been chatting to Jordan again, have you?' Peter enquired with a touch of sharpness as he released her,

'I was just keeping Madeleine company until you got back,' Jordan put in, his tone once more light and casual, every emotion smoothed from it. 'But now I think it's time I was going. Where's your mother? I'd like to say goodnight to her.'

'She's over there somewhere.'

Peter waved a vague hand, using his superior height to peer over the heads of the people near them in search of his mother. He was very close to Jordan as he spoke, and Madeleine was struck once more by the way Peter's conventional handsomeness had no impact on her. It was Jordan's face that drew her gaze and held it; she found greater depths and more to appeal to her in the strong-boned features each time she looked at him. Attractiveness was a hard thing to define but, where Peter was merely good-looking, Jordan's attraction had a force that took her breath away.

With a quiver of reaction she recognised what was happening to her, why she had been drawn to Jordan from the start and why she felt this sensitivity towards him that was so much greater than it had ever been with anyone else. Jordan was the sort of man she could quite easily fall in love with; in fact, she was not at all sure that she wasn't more than half in love with him already.

'Moved your horses into Northcote yet, Jordy?' Peter was saying and, as Madeleine saw the flicker of anger across Jordan's face at the nickname, she suddenly realised that alone of all her acquaintants he was the only one who continued to use her own full name, never changing it to the Maddy she so disliked.

'They arrive on Tuesday.' Unexpectedly, Jordan turned his head in Madeleine's direction. 'Perhaps you'd like to come up to the Hall some time and see what we're doing to the place. If you come next weekend you can see the horses, too.'

The invitation came so offhandedly that no one listening would have attached any importance to it, but to Madeleine it was as if a door had suddenly opened in those steel walls that surrounded Jordan. She didn't know why he had offered the invitation, she only knew she had to accept it.

'I'd like that very much.'

She couldn't have kept the delight from her eyes and her voice if she'd tried, but she didn't even try, wanting

Jordan to see how much the small olive branch he held out to her had meant.

'Saturday, perhaps, if you're free. I'll phone you during the week. Perhaps we can continue our— talk——' the word was emphasised with faint irony '—if you still want to.'

And while Madeleine was still wondering exactly how to take that final, double-edged remark, he tossed a casual goodbye at Peter and shouldered his way through the crowd, his uneven stride making it easy to follow his progress.

'What talk?' Peter had caught the emphasis on that last comment.

'Oh——' Madeleine dragged her eyes from the back of Jordan's head to meet Peter's irritated blue gaze. 'I told you, he was telling me about his horses.'

A scowl darkened the handsome features. 'Why the sudden interest in horses, Maddy? I seem to recall that you told me they bored you rigid—and I don't like the idea of my girl associating with another man.'

'It's none of your business!' She had been about to make some vague comment on the lines of the fact that she had come to see that there was more to the subject than she realised, but once more that possessive 'my girl' jarred, driving her to an angry retort before she had time to think. 'And I am *not* your girl!'

'You're here with me tonight.'

'But you don't own me! I'm a free agent, I can go where I please, see who I please.'

'It's Jordan, isn't it?' Peter's tone was the easiest one in the world to read. He was jealous. Dear lord, this was all she needed!

'Peter——' she began protestingly, but Peter cut in on her.

'Don't let him kid you, Maddy. He's not all he makes himself out to be, you know.'

'In what way, exactly?' Madeleine's voice was tart. Jordan had never made himself out to 'be' anything.

'In any way. Riding, for instance.'

So the jealousy wasn't just over her. Peter envied Jordan his success, too.

'I know he lost his place on the Olympic team because of his accident,' she said wearily. In this mood Peter was very tiresome.

'That's not all he lost.' Peter looked positively triumphant, almost gloating.

'Peter, what *are* you talking about?'

'His nerve. That fall broke Jordan's nerve, as well as his leg. He's never been back on a horse since.'

'But the doctors——'

'Doctors, garbage!' Peter interrupted rudely. 'That's just an excuse. Jordan's finished and he knows it. He'll never ride again.'

'No!' Madeleine gazed dazedly up into the face of the man before her. 'That can't be true!' Riding, horses—they were Jordan's life. The accident couldn't have destroyed that. 'I don't believe you!' she declared vehemently, knowing from the swift look he shot her that she had confirmed his suspicions about herself where Jordan was concerned, but she was past caring.

'Don't believe me,' Peter sneered, his handsome face suddenly ugly with contempt. 'Put your faith in whatever lies he's told you—but Jordan Sumner is finished—*kaput*! Oh, don't take my word for it—go to Northcote, talk to Michael, he'll tell you. Or if Mick's too damn loyal to admit his brother's blown it, ask Sukey.'

'S-Sukey?'

Somehow Madeleine dragged up the extra reserves of strength needed to switch her reaction to Peter's words from one that betrayed her stunned recognition of the name to blank curiosity.

'Who's Sukey?'

Peter's laugh was an ugly sound. Dear God, but he had clearly been stewing in his jealousy for years!

'The one before you. Jordan's girlfriend—lover, mistress—call her what you like. Whatever she was, she's regretting it like hell now.'

'Why?' It came out on a shaky gasp.

'He screwed her up completely, that's why. When she met him she was just seventeen, fresh out of school and very innocent—naïve, I suppose you could say. She certainly didn't know how to handle someone like Jordan. He seduced her, wound her round his little finger, and then when she was head over heels in love with him he dropped her like that.' Peter snapped his fingers to emphasise his point.

'But people change. They fall in and out of love.' Hadn't she once believed she was deeply in love with Viv, only to find that the whole thing had been a terrible mistake? 'Jordan couldn't help it if his feelings changed. He had to tell her——'

'In public?' Peter scorned. 'In the collecting ring at the bloody Horse of the Year Show? When she was pregnant with his child?' he continued inexorably.

'How—how do you know all this?' Madeleine's voice came and went uncontrollably. Could Jordan really have been so callous? Her heart wanted to deny the idea, but her head reminded her of the other side to Jordan, the darker, dangerous side to him that had emerged that night in her car on the journey back to the Manor. That man could have treated Sukey in this way.

'Gerry heard the story from someone who was there, and I met the poor kid at Badminton. She'd gone there to try and see Jordan, but of course he avoided her like the plague. I got talking to her at a party—she was rather drunk and she told me the whole story—cried her eyes out over me.'

'And—the baby?' Madeleine forced herself to ask.

'She had an abortion.' The words fell like blows on Madeleine's sensitive nerves. 'And now he doesn't even acknowledge that she exists. That's how much he cares for people, Maddy, so remember that if you still think you want him. He'll discard you without a second thought when he's tired of you, just as he did to Sukey. He won't care if he hurts you—horses have his heart— if he's got one, which I doubt.'

And, try as she might, that was something Madeleine couldn't refute. Hadn't she already admitted to herself that Jordan seemed to put his horses first, before any other consideration? Unwillingly she thought back over Jordan's behaviour on the terrace. She had thought, had even told him, that his reaction was that of a man who had been hurt, but couldn't it also be interpreted as the behaviour of someone who had discarded a lover like a piece of rotten fruit, and was angry at the thought that that person might still be trying to get in touch? It was a bitter irony that only minutes before she had been so happy at Jordan's invitation to Northcote, seeing it as a chance to get closer to him at last, but now she was no longer sure she wanted that closeness at all.

Her head throbbed, the ache she had pretended to earlier now becoming a reality, she felt exhausted and thought longingly of going home and burying all her doubts and uncertainty in the oblivion of sleep, but there was one more question that had to be asked.

'Did you tell Sukey that Jordan had moved to Northcote?'

'As a matter of fact, I did,' Peter responded carelessly. 'And I offered her a room here, too, if she ever needed it.'

'Why do I get the impression that last night wasn't exactly an unqualified success?' Lucina Crawford enquired half-way through a morning in which Madeleine had been so abrupt with two customers that she had driven them away without buying anything, had given change for five pounds when she had actually been offered ten, and finally, in an attack of uncharacteristic clumsiness, had sent one of the commemorative beakers from Northcote flying to the floor where it had smashed into tiny, irreparable slivers of china.

'Oh, Mum, it was dreadful!'

Madeleine looked up from the dustpan into which she was sweeping the remnants of the shattered beaker, her eyes dull with lack of sleep and the strain of her thoughts in the darkness of her bedroom. She had hardly stopped thinking since Peter had grudgingly driven her home, an uncomfortably silent journey, at the end of which he had driven off again without so much as a goodbye. She had lain awake for much of the night, going over and over everything Peter had said, going round in circles and getting nowhere, only falling asleep just as dawn was breaking.

On her mother's desk, the telephone hiccuped and then shrilled into sound. Lucina reached out a hand to lift the receiver.

'Crawford Antiques. Good morning, can I help you?' She paused, listening. 'Certainly, who's calling, please? Oh, yes, just a minute.' She held the receiver out to

Madeleine. 'For you—a Mr Sumner. Isn't he the man you took to Northcote?'

Madeleine nodded silently, her palms suddenly damp with perspiration. Jordan had said he would contact her, but she had only half believed him, and she hadn't expected his call quite so soon. She wasn't ready to talk to him, the things Peter had said were still too raw in her mind. Her heart thudded painfully against her ribs as she took the receiver from her mother.

'Hello, Jordan.'

'Good morning, Madeleine. I'm ringing to ask if you still want to come up to Northcote this weekend.' Jordan's tone was crisp and businesslike. 'I have to go to Buckinghamshire later today to help load up the horses and travel back with them tomorrow, and after that I'm going to be hellishly busy, so I thought I'd get the details sorted out, then there's one thing I can forget about.'

It was all very reasonable, but all the same it stung to think she was something he wanted out of the way so that he could forget about her, and she didn't know what to say about his invitation. Yesterday she had been over-joyed at the thought of a trip to Northcote, but that had been before Peter had told her the truth about Sukey. Now she was not so sure. Did she want to go or not?

'Madeleine?' She had been silent too long, she had to give him an answer.

'You said Saturday.' Madeleine hated the sound of her voice; it was stilted and stiff, betraying her uncertainty. 'That's my day off this week. I could come then.'

She wanted to see the alterations, she told herself, she was interested to see what Jordan had done with the Hall. But she didn't convince herself; deep down she knew she had to see Jordan again, even if rational thought told her that, after what she had heard from Peter, she would be safer to stay away.

'Saturday will be fine, say, two-thirty? Mick—my brother—will be here by then.'

Now why had he added that? Simply as casual conversation, or to imply that there would be a third party there to defuse the situation, a chaperon?

'I'd like to meet him. Is he very like you?'

A tiny pause. Was Jordan, too, thinking carefully about everything he said?

'Not at all. Mick's very much the family man. Look, sorry to rush you, but I must go. I'll see you Saturday.'

'Saturday,' Madeleine confirmed. 'I'll look forward to it.' But Jordan had already replaced the receiver, and only the hum of the dialling tone greeted her words.

For a moment Madeleine stared at the instrument in her hand. She was committed now, unless she rang up with some fake story about being unwell—but she knew she would not do that. She was going to Northcote; she knew she was incapable of staying away.

'Jordan Sumner,' Lucina Crawford said thoughtfully. 'Is *he* the one who keeps you awake at nights?'

Startled, Madeleine looked straight into her mother's turquoise eyes, seeing in them deep sympathy and understanding.

'You know?'

Lucina nodded gently. 'My bedroom *is* next to yours. I couldn't miss the number of times your light's gone on in the middle of the night, the trips downstairs to make a drink. If you're thinking about him, they can't be happy thoughts.'

'They're not. Oh, Mum——'

And suddenly it was all spilling out, the meeting with Jordan, the argument in the car, the Ball and Peter's hateful revelations at the end of it. Lucina waited silently until her daughter finally stumbled to a halt.

'And how do you feel?' she asked quietly.

'I—I don't know,' Madeleine answered honestly. 'I just know that Jordan is somehow different from every other man I've ever met—he's touched me in a way that's totally outside anything I've ever experienced before.' She couldn't mention the feeling she had had the night before, the admission that Jordan was the sort of man she could easily fall in love with. That was too new and uncertain to be communicated to anyone, even her mother. Besides, Peter's account of Jordan's treatment of Sukey had threatened that delicate, new-found feeling. 'I know it would probably be safer never to see Jordan again, but I just can't!'

Lucina nodded slowly. 'I know just how you feel. I felt like that about your father the first time I met him—I always did, even after he'd left and gone to live somewhere else. But I've never regretted the time I spent with him, and I know I never will. Love is never wasted, no matter how it ends. I can't tell you if it will work for you, darling, I only know that we all have an instinct—a sort of sixth sense that tells us when someone is important in our lives, and our days would be poorer if we didn't act on that instinct. Use your intuition, Madeleine. If it's telling you that this Jordan is somehow special to you, then follow it and don't give up until you find out why.'

'If it's telling you that this Jordan is somehow special...' Her mother's words echoed in Madeleine's head long after she had returned to work, unsettling her mind and making it extremely difficult to concentrate on anything. That was exactly what her instincts *were* telling her, and because of that she viewed the coming visit to Northcote with strong apprehension, her nervousness made all the worse by the knowledge that the tension that clenched her stomach muscles at the thought of Saturday's meeting came not only from uncertainty as to what Jordan's reaction would be when he saw her again, but also from the fear of knowing just how important he might eventually come to be.

CHAPTER NINE

MADELEINE saw Jordan as soon as her Mini swung up the curve of the drive and on to the gravel at the front of Northcote Hall, and immediately the feeling, like a thousand butterflies beating their wings frantically inside her stomach, intensified, setting her nerves tingling as she watched him make his limping way towards her. Unthinkingly she raised her hand to wave a greeting, only to lower it again in a fury of confusion, uncertain as to her welcome.

'I'm sorry I'm late,' she began as soon as she was within earshot. 'Minnie here has been playing up, she wouldn't start for ages. It was the same last week, but I thought that was just the damp weather.'

Becoming aware of how her nervous tongue was running away with her, she coloured fiercely, flashed a bright, uneasy smile, and announced with false cheerfulness, 'Well, I'm here now!'

'So you are,' was the laconic response, no answering smile lighting Jordan's face.

Madeleine's heart plummeted sharply. This was not an auspicious beginning. Jordan looked as if he had himself on a very tight rein, as if he had worked out each word, each expression, possibly even each thought. She shouldn't have waited until today to come, she should have used the small advantage the night of the Ball had given her and driven to Northcote as soon as Jordan had got back from Buckinghamshire. He had had almost a week in which to rebuild his defences, rein-

124

force the steel shutters, and now it seemed as if only a full-scale atomic explosion could breach them.

'Would you like to look around the house or the stables first? Or perhaps you'd like something to drink——'

'No, thanks, I had coffee just before I left.'

Madeleine's response came automatically; she had scarcely heard Jordan's words. Her eyes and her mind were busy drinking in the sight and the sound of him after what seemed like a lifetime of separation, in spite of the fact that it had only been a few days.

He looked better, physically, at least. The pallor of his face was less pronounced, and he seemed to have put on a little weight, relieving the almost painful thinness that had struck her so forcefully at their first meeting. He was casually dressed in denim jeans, and a dark grey sweatshirt that mirrored the smoky colour of his eyes, the soft material clinging to the firm muscles of his chest and shoulders. His hair had grown slightly too, revealing that wayward tendency to wave that she had suspected would appear, and even such slight sunlight as they had been blessed with that spring had touched it softly, adding a glint of gold to the honey-brown.

Perhaps it was the play of mild sunlight across those hard-boned features, or perhaps it was her recent admission to herself that this man was coming to mean something very special to her, but suddenly Madeleine was intensely aware of Jordan's physical presence in a way that made her realise that his impact had only ever reached her in a weakened form before, diluted by the confusion of her own feelings.

His slim body was deceptive, he was like a hunting animal, fined down to essentials, every line honed to perfection by years of training. She was overwhelmed by a longing to reach out and touch him, feel those corded muscles slide under her fingertips, tangle her hands in the sun-kissed crispness of his hair. When he shifted his stance to ease his damaged leg, the movement drew the worn denim of his jeans tight over powerful thighs in a way that heated the blood in Madeleine's veins, drying her throat so that she had to swallow sharply to relieve it. A stray breeze stirred his hair, sending a lock of it over his forehead, and he lifted one of those deceptively elegant hands to push it back impatiently.

Madeleine's eyes followed the small movement as if mesmerised, unable to suppress the longing to know what it would feel like to have those hands touch her body, to know their power used to please rather than to control or hurt, as she had already experienced. It came as a jarring shock to realise that she had never even felt that firm mouth on hers. She had felt so intimately involved with Jordan that it was as if they had already been lovers for some time.

'So, what's it to be—the house or the stables?'

Jordan played the affable host almost to perfection. If it wasn't for the sensitivity of every nerve-end, Madeleine might have been convinced by it. But that fluttering of butterfly wings in her stomach, the stinging pins-and-needles sensation on her skin, kept her aware of everything that was being carefully left unsaid, the subjects they were both avoiding, and with Peter's sneering voice ringing in her ears she shifted uncomfortably where she stood, unable to meet that direct, emotionless gaze with any degree of equanimity. She was here, she wanted to be here, unable to deny the pull of Jordan's attraction, but, remembering the story of his callous treatment of Sukey, she suddenly wished she had never come. It was foolish and dangerous, exposing herself to the risk of similar treatment.

'The stables, I think,' she said, controlling her voice with an effort. 'While we've got some sunshine it seems a pity to go inside.'

'The stables it is, then.' Jordan shot a swift, considering look at her feet. 'At least you're wearing sensible shoes. We'd have had to find some boots for you otherwise.'

'I did think about that.' And she'd done more than think. Faint colour washed Madeleine's cheeks at the memory of how she had agonised over what to wear this afternoon. She had tried several outfits and discarded them, finally deciding to opt for practicality in navy cord jeans, with a lighter blue shirt sprigged with tiny white flowers worn under a matching quilted waistcoat. She had caught her hair into a casual ponytail and the dark silky mane hung half-way down her back. 'You said you'd show me the horses, so...'

Her voice faltered and died, ending with an embarrassing croak as Jordan's eyes moved from her feet and upwards over the rest of her body, the slow survey unnerving her, recalling memories of an almost identical moment at the Ball and making her palms damp with nervous perspiration at the thought of the unexpected burning desire she had seen in his eyes then. How would she feel if she saw the same passion there now?

Her mind seemed to split in two, one half admitting that that was what she wanted most in the whole world, the other crying a warning that she couldn't handle that. Did she want to end up like poor, gullible Sukey, cast aside without a second thought when Jordan tired of her? Without thinking, she wiped her hands on the soft cord that covered her thighs and immediately wished she hadn't as she saw the swift flicker of those silvery eyes follow the movement. She shivered involuntarily, and at once the tension of the moment was shattered as Jordan frowned his concern.

'You're getting cold. We'd better move.'

Madeleine couldn't tell if relief or despair was uppermost in her mind, because the eyes that lifted to her own showed nothing more than a polite care for her comfort. A moment later he was heading towards the stables, leaving her to stumble along in his wake, her mind a turmoil of doubts and questions.

Had she imagined that moment at the Ball? she wondered dazedly. Had she misread his expression completely, seeing in it the response she had wanted rather than what was actually there? Silently she scorned her earlier fears. There was no danger of her being cast aside as Sukey had been; Jordan had no interest in her in that way at all. But the thought brought no comfort; instead there was a dreary ache of loss deep inside her.

By exerting a great deal of mental effort, Madeleine found that, by the time they reached the cobblestoned courtyard that formed the centre of the stable block, she had managed to regain enough composure to enable her to take an interest in and absorb some of what Jordan told her as he led her past the loose-boxes that formed three sides of a square, the fourth being the wall of the Hall itself. She was helped by the fact that she really wanted to learn as much as she possibly could about this world that was so vital a part of Jordan's life and which, until now, had always been a completely closed book to her.

So she listened, and found it easy to learn because Jordan was obviously a master of his subject, able to explain the basic facts in a clear, concise way, occasionally with a flash of dry humour or some story that made each horse a character and a personality in its own right, and not just the rather awesome creature Madeleine had at first believed it to be. Her head was reeling with terms like girth, snaffle and curb after a visit to the tack room. Then they reached the set of stalls that housed Michael Sumner's show jumpers where, in the last loose-box, they came across Jordan's brother himself, grooming a dark bay mare.

Michael was exactly Jordan's height, though broader in build, which gave him a stocky appearance in contrast to his brother's slim strength. His hair and eyes were several shades darker, but all the same there was no denying the obvious close relationship, though Michael's rounder face was totally without the austerity that marked Jordan's so strongly. As Jordan performed the introductions, Michael tossed the brush he had been using on to a pile of straw and, pushing past the mare's powerful hindquarters with a confidence Madeleine secretly envied, came to the stable door.

'It's good to meet a local at last,' he grinned, extending a rather grubby, square-fingered hand. 'I've been here five days and you're the first neighbour I've seen.'

'Hardly a neighbour,' Madeleine laughed, her spirits lifting in response to Michael's easy friendliness, which was such a contrast to Jordan's carefully distanced formality. Michael's handshake had a firm strength that matched his brother's, but a handshake was all it was. There were no worrying sensations of heightened sensitivity to disturb her when she touched his hand. 'Holtby is fifteen miles away.'

'Near enough.' Michael dismissed the distance nonchalantly. 'I'm just glad to see a new face. Jordan's told me a lot about you. You don't ride, do you?'

Madeleine could only shake her head, her mind filled with questions she couldn't ask. Just what had Jordan told his brother about her? She slid a glance at Jordan's face, but his expression told her nothing.

'Oh well, I won't hold that against you. Perhaps Jordan will give you lessons if you ask him nicely—he's an excellent teacher, if a bit of a slave-driver. He knocked me into shape for Badminton all right.'

'I understand you're to be congratulated on doing so well.' Jordan's surprised glance had Madeleine explaining hastily, 'Peter told me.'

'Ah yes, dear Peter.' A conspiratorial glance passed between the two brothers. 'But I didn't do very much. I just sat on Diamond, closed my eyes and prayed every time we came to a fence—I don't have Jordan's genius when it comes to cross-country riding. Have you met the stars of the show yet?'

'He means my horses,' Jordan put in, seeing Madeleine's puzzled frown. 'I'm just taking Madeleine there now,' he added to Michael. 'Are you finished here?'

'Almost—another ten minutes should see it done. Then I'm going to make a pot of tea—I could murder a cuppa. I'll see you in about half an hour, Madeleine, if you can drag Jordan away from his beloved darlings by then.'

Michael's last remark sent a sensation like the trickle of icy water down Madeleine's spine, as it awoke unwelcome echoes of Peter's damning description of Jordan as heartless except where horses were concerned. She had been enjoying the afternoon in Jordan's company, forgetful of the complications of Sukey and Jordan's treatment of her, but the memory seemed to cast a shadow over the day, one that grew darker as she saw the way Jordan's expression softened perceptibly at the sight of the first of his 'beloved darlings', a showy and, to Madeleine's mind, frighteningly large chestnut stallion. Something twisted painfully inside her as she saw the warmth that came into his eyes.

Would she ever see that controlled mask break into that gentle smile just for her? She winced mentally at the stabbing pain that told her just how much that meant, burning tears blurring her vision as Jordan's long-fingered hand went out to stroke the enquiring nose that was pushed into it.

'The mare's proper name is Starlight Solitaire and this fellow's Autumn Flame,' Jordan explained. 'But to us they're just Diamond and Flame. Okay, greedy!' The words were directed at the horse, Jordan's laugh a warm, rich sound that tore at Madeleine's heart with a savage sense of loss as he pulled some chunks of apple from his pocket and fed them to the stallion, slapping an affectionate hand against the animal's strong neck.

A rustle in the straw drew Madeleine's attention. Inside the stall she saw a large black and white cat emerge from the piled up bedding and stretch lazily. Immediately Flame swung round, making her cry out in alarm.

'Don't panic.' A trace of laughter lingered in Jordan's voice.' They're great friends, stable companions, in fact. The Snig goes everywhere with Flame.'

'The what?' Madeleine's voice sounded breathless; the smile that curved Jordan's lips was having a devastating effect on her pulse-rate.

'The Snig. Mick gave him his name, it's a dialect word meaning a baby eel, and if you look you'll see why——'

Jordan caught hold of Madeleine's arm to draw her closer to the half-door of the stall. Peering into the dim light, she saw the cat wind itself sinuously in and out of the horse's legs, purring ecstatically. As she watched, transfixed, the chestnut lowered his head to push gently at the black and white fur.

'That's beautiful! They trust each other completely!'

Madeleine turned to Jordan in delight, her smile fading abruptly as she realised how close they were, his hand still on her arm, their faces almost touching in the confined opening. For a long, taut moment their eyes met and held, and her heart turned over as she saw the sudden flare of fire in his eyes. Then, with a start, she pulled back and away, finding his proximity too disturbing to bear. She regretted the impulsive movement immediately, as she saw the light fade from his eyes, leaving them clouded and opaque once more. With an aching sense of regret, she watched the distant mask slip back into place as Jordan, with a final pat on the sleek chestnut neck, moved on to the next stall.

After Flame's dramatic size and strength, the black mare, with just a tiny white star on her forehead that clearly gave her her name, seemed almost small by comparison, but Jordan warned Madeleine not to be deceived by her appearance.

'Flame might have the looks, but this lady does the hard work. She's a real trier—she'll have a go at anything I—Mick—puts her at.'

The hesitation was slight, but it was there and Madeleine felt something tug at her heart as she recalled Peter's gloating declaration that Jordan had lost his nerve. It didn't seem possible, seeing the absorbed, relaxed pleasure on his face as he fed the mare a chunk of apple. The gentleness with which Diamond took the treat from Jordan's upturned palm encouraged her to ask impulsively, 'Could I do that?'

Silently Jordan handed her a section of the fruit, but when she would have held it out with her fingers curled upwards he moved forward, taking her hand in his and smoothing her fingers flat.

'Always keep your hand like that,' he said quietly. 'That way she won't mistake one of your fingers for a tasty titbit.'

As he spoke, he drew her nearer to the mare, supporting the back of her hand in his palm so that he must have felt her tension as the horse's head came towards her.

'She won't hurt you,' he added reassuringly, and Madeleine had to bite her lower lip hard against the nervous laugh that almost escaped her. The feeling that strung every nerve tight as a coiled spring had nothing to do with fear of the mare who had now taken the apple delicately, but was her response to the touch of Jordan's hand on her own. A fierce need shot through her at the brush of his skin against hers, heating her blood so that she trembled uncontrollably, the ground seeming suddenly insecure beneath her. She wanted to turn to Jordan, let her feelings show in her face so that he would know, but the memory of Peter's words held her back so that she took refuge in trivia instead.

'She was so gentle,' she said with an uncertain little gesture in the direction of the black mare, 'and she doesn't even know me.'

'She knows you won't hurt her.' Jordan's voice was low and slightly rough. 'Animals have a sixth sense about such things.'

Madeleine's breath caught in her throat, as an echo of her mother's words sprang into her mind.

'Some humans have that, too,' she said unevenly, and suddenly everything they were avoiding saying welled up inside her like a flood-tide breaking through a dam that could no longer contain it. 'Jordan—I know about Sukey now—Peter told me—he met her at Badminton and she——' Meeting those suspiciously narrowed silver eyes, she had to force herself to go on. 'She told him everything.'

'*Everything?*'

The single word sliced through the air, a world of meaning behind it. Jordan's eyes were as cold and hard as the cobblestones in the courtyard, but Madeleine was determined to clear away the misunderstanding between them and she refused to let his withdrawal deter her.

'I—don't know.' What *was* everything? Wasn't what Peter had told her enough? Enough to warn you to keep away, a small voice inside her head told her, but she was committed now, she couldn't go back. 'But, Jordan, don't you see—*Peter* told Sukey you were here, not me. He and Rupert knew about her all the time. That's how I knew her name, I overheard Gerry talking about her at the antiques fair...'

Once more her voice failed her. Apart from that one, stabbing reaction, Jordan had made no response at all. Heavy lids hooded his eyes once more, closing them off from her. She wished he would say something. Couldn't he see how much she needed to know how he felt?

'Jordan——' she began again hesitantly, but Jordan cut in on her sharply.

'God knows, I want to believe you!' he declared harshly. 'When you look at me like this I can't help but believe you!'

Her hand was still in his and, without warning, he suddenly pulled her towards him, dragging her close up against the firm strength of his body. His left hand crept up to cradle her cheek, lifting her face to his, his eyes so burningly intent they were almost translucent.

'I want to believe you, Madeleine,' he muttered huskily. 'You can't know how much I want it—it frightens me when I think how much it would mean to be able to trust you.'

Madeleine found she was having trouble breathing. Her heart was beating high up in her throat, making her gasp for air as she twisted her hand in Jordan's, until she was gripping his fingers with a strength she hadn't known she possessed.

'You *can* believe me, Jordan. You have to believe me!'

She saw the change in his face, the swift darkening of his eyes, and knew it was mirrored in her own. They both knew what was going to happen and neither of them tried to fight it. It was right and natural, and Madeleine at least had been waiting for this for a long, long time.

Jordan's lips were warm and firm, but gentle, the soft brush of his kiss delicate and almost tentative. But then, as if that tiny touch had swept aside the restraints that had come between them, he deepened the caress, moving from subtle persuasion to tenderness to a forceful urgency in the space of a heartbeat. Madeleine followed him without hesitation, letting her mouth open under his, meeting his demands with her own until she was lost in sensation, drowning in a longing to be near to this man, to give everything she possessed to him, her heart, her mind and, as the flickering fire crept through her, obliterating all thought of her own safety, of Peter's warning, she knew the desire to give him the final gift of herself.

Jordan's hand was at her head, entangling in the brown silk of her hair, the other smoothing the lines of her body, adding fuel to the burning need inside her. When his fingers slid inside her blouse at its open neck, she strained against him, murmuring his name on a sobbing sigh of surrender as she felt the hardness of his hand on the soft swell of her breast.

Her mind hazy with longing, she barely heard Jordan's harsh intake of breath or felt his sudden tension, but a moment later his mouth was wrenched away from her, his head lifted and, heedless of her wordless cry of protest, he put her from him abruptly, his hands lingering for a second only to steady her when she would have stumbled, then falling to his sides. The distance between them was suddenly so great that Madeleine felt her heart would tear in two at the separation.

'I didn't mean that to happen,' Jordan muttered in a voice that was rough and thick with ill-concealed emotion. 'It won't happen again.' Then, as Madeleine simply stared, her eyes wide blue pools of distress, he added unevenly, 'I'm sorry.'

The two words shattered Madeleine's control completely.

'You're sorry!' she repeated in a voice that was high and sharp with pain. 'You're *sorry*! Damn you, Jordan, what sort of a response is that? Can't you feel? Did I react like someone who would want you to *apologise*?'

There was no life in those stony grey eyes or the hard, set face. Madeleine could almost hear the slam of the steel doors.

'It won't happen again,' Jordan stated harshly and it sounded like a command, though whether to her or himself Madeleine couldn't gauge. Then, with one of those disturbing switches of mood, he assumed once more the carefully controlled mask of the polite host. 'It's time we went inside. Mick will be waiting.'

Madeleine wanted to dig her heels in, refuse to go anywhere, but something in his face forced her to bite back her words of angry protest. She didn't know what had brought about the change in him, the swift transition from burning passion to this deliberate, rigid distance; she only knew the pain that tore at her heart at the loss of what she had wanted so much.

'You still don't trust me,' she said softly, unhappily. 'I told you the truth, but you still don't believe me.'

She was looking straight into his eyes as she spoke, and saw him blink just once in stunned bewilderment. Then, after that one tiny reaction, Jordan's next move was silent and totally unexpected. One strong hand reached out and touched her face, tracing the lines that pain had drawn around her eyes with infinite gentleness.

'I think we have some talking to do,' he said slowly. 'But not yet——'

'Then when?' Sorrow, hope and impatience tangled up in each other in her voice and Jordan's expression lightened fractionally at her tone.

'Not now.' It was a sigh of tiredness and resignation. 'Mick will be wondering where we've got to.'

A strand of dark hair had come free from her ponytail, pulled loose by Jordan's caressing fingers, and now he hooked it behind her ear with a gentleness that made her eyes burn with unshed tears. *Soon,* she cried silently in her mind, make it soon!

'Not yet, Madeleine,' Jordan said quietly, but with a firmness that prevented further argument. 'I don't have Diamond's ability to trust on instinct—or yours either, for that matter. But be patient, give me time, and perhaps we'll get there in the end.'

CHAPTER TEN

IT WASN'T easy to be patient, to chat about trivia when all the things Madeleine really wanted to say were burning in her brain as if etched there in white-hot flames. But Michael's friendly presence eased the atmosphere, and the tension of waiting. Responding to his fatherly need to talk about his two young sons, left behind with their mother until certain essential repairs turned Northcote into a suitable home for them, Madeleine found that the time slipped away without her quite being aware of it passing. She also went on a tour of the house to inspect the alterations, and, remembering the eyesore the Evensleighs had created out of the Manor, she was relieved and delighted to find that both Jordan and Michael were determined to preserve the character of the old Hall, and the modernisations were kept carefully within the original atmosphere of the house.

The conversation ranged far and wide, Jordan and his brother contributing equally to maintaining its easy flow, and in the space of an hour Madeleine learned more about the world of horses and riding than she would have thought possible. Jordan even opened up on the subject of his own career, and she listened, fascinated, as he and Michael shared reminiscences, giving her an insight into a subject that until now had been a closed book to her.

At last Michael sighed, stretched and, declaring there was no peace for the wicked, levered himself out of his armchair to organise the evening exercise for the horses.

'I don't know how I'm going to manage with only half the stablehands here,' he grumbled. Then a thought struck him and he glanced across at Madeleine. 'I don't suppose you fancy a ride?'

Madeleine's instinctive response was to shake her head vehemently, but then she remembered Diamond's gentleness when she had taken the apple and stilled the gesture. Why not?

'Madeleine's never ridden before.' It was Jordan who intervened, a sharp warning note in his voice.

'Oh, come off it, Jordan!' Michael protested. 'I'll put her on Dove—she's a real old Dobbin of a horse.'

'I'd like to try,' Madeleine put in impulsively and, surprisingly, truthfully. She found she very much wanted to try this experience that meant so much to Jordan. 'Please.'

Jordan's eyes probed hers, she could feel his doubt and tension tightening her own muscles.

'You can't go alone,' he said, just when she was convinced he would refuse to agree, adding unexpectedly, 'I'll come with you.'

'Jordan——' Michael's voice echoed the shock that filled Madeleine's mind, his eyes asking a question without words. With Peter's sneering comments about Jordan's loss of nerve ringing in her head, Madeleine held her breath and waited. Dark grey eyes locked with silver ones, and apparently Michael found the answer he wanted in his brother's face for he shrugged and said quietly, 'If you're sure.'

'Start with the basics and build up slowly, that's what the doctor said.'

Jordan's light tone might have deceived a less sensitive listener, but Madeleine caught the underlying unevenness, and it combined with Michael's unconcealed anxiety to make her regret her uncharacteristic impulsiveness and wish her unguarded words back. But it was too late; already Jordan was on his feet and heading towards the door.

He seemed relaxed enough as he went about the business of saddling the horses, Madeleine having plenty of time to watch him as she stood back from a procedure she didn't understand, leaving it to the experts. Perhaps the well known routine was so automatic that he didn't have to stop and think about it, his strong hands with that strange back-to-front movement fastening buckles, tightening girths and adjusting stirrups with the ease of long practice. But Madeleine had too much time to think, to reflect on what all this might mean and the possible repercussions for Jordan if something went wrong, so that by the time they were ready to mount she was trembling with nerves.

'Are you OK?' Jordan asked when he saw her face. 'Mick's right, you know,' he went on, misinterpreting the reasons for her disturbed state, 'Dove's just a plodder. She's a very old lady—she was Mick's first horse, so we keep her for sentimental reasons. But if you're really worried you can always back out, no one will mind.'

Silently Madeleine shook her head. She was determined to go through with this and, really, she was past thinking about herself. If Jordan had finally overcome whatever mental block had prevented him riding since his accident, she wasn't going to give in now and risk his deciding that, as her host, his place was to stay behind with her.

Her last thought as Jordan gave her a leg-up into the saddle was that it was lucky she had decided to wear her jeans. After that, every coherent thought fled from her mind at the realisation of exactly what she had let herself in for. With a convulsive gulp she gathered up the reins, struggling to concentrate on Jordan's instructions as he showed her how to hold them properly.

'One in each hand—hold them between the thumb and the first fingers with your thumbs nearer her head.'

Madeleine risked a glance at Dove's grey head directly in front of her, the horse's ears pricked and alert. Dove's back seemed incredibly wide, Madeleine's legs were stretched uncomfortably tightly and the ground seemed a long, long way away.

Concentrating hard, she didn't see the moment when Jordan swung himself into the saddle, though half her mind noted that he had chosen to ride the chestnut Flame and not the smaller, quieter Diamond, as she had expected. But then she remembered Geraldine's comment about Swallow's colouring, and she guessed intuitively that Jordan had avoided Diamond because her black coat reminded him too sharply of the horse he had been riding on the day of his accident, whose fall had crushed his leg. A moment later Flame moved forward, the leading rein attached to Dove's bridle, its other end held firmly in Jordan's right hand, tightened and, with a clatter of hooves on the cobbles, they were off and all her attention was concentrated on the disturbing swaying movement of the animal beneath her.

For some time, it was all she could do to make sure she stayed put, and resist the craven impulse to grasp Dove's mane and cling on for dear life. But very slowly she adjusted and even gained a little confidence, and then, much to her own astonishment, she discovered she was actually enjoying the experience. It was only then that she dared to risk a sidelong glance at Jordan's face, and she was thoroughly disconcerted to find that he was watching her closely.

'You're doing very well.' The quiet voice was encouraging. 'Just relax and don't pull on the reins. Dove will take care of you.'

Just for the moment the old Jordan, the man she had felt such empathy with, was back, and Madeleine felt a pulse beating high up in her throat as she managed a half-hearted smile in response to his words. She felt she would have done anything, even ridden the powerful Flame, if it would bring that warmth to his eyes. She studied Jordan covertly from beneath her eyelashes. He seemed so controlled, every movement easy and relaxed, the faint sheen of perspiration on his face the only indication of any inner tension. Surely it couldn't be that easy! But then she was forgetting that, as she had learned that afternoon, Jordan had first been put on a horse when he was two years old. After a lifetime's experience, she supposed that the skill of riding became instinctive, like driving or swimming.

She had been concentrating so hard that she hadn't noticed how far they had ridden. Ahead of them, Michael and the grooms were turning and trotting back towards them. As his brother drew alongside, Madeleine saw the swift change in Jordan's face, but before she had even had time to try to interpret what his expression meant he had tossed the leading rein in Michael's direction with a muttered, 'Look after Madeleine for me.'

And before Michael had time to voice the protest that was clearly forming on his lips, Jordan had swung Flame away from them, pressing his heels against the chestnut's sides and urging him into a gallop that had Madeleine catching her breath in fear and dismay.

'Jordan—no!' Madeleine and Michael spoke simultaneously, stopped, and their eyes met in a second's understanding of each other's concern. Then, abruptly, Michael shrugged.

'Let him go,' he said quietly. 'This had to come some time, and I suppose now is as good as time as any. One thing's for sure,' he added, turning to watch the chestnut's furious gallop, 'there'll be no going back after this. It's a case of kill or cure.'

Madeleine could have wished that he'd phrased his comment differently; his words combined with her memories of Geraldine's account of Jordan's accident to send a cold shiver down her spine. But when she too turned to watch Jordan, she found such gloomy thoughts were driven from her head as her gaze was caught and held entranced by the spectacle in front of her.

She had always appreciated the physical beauty of a horse in motion, but never before had she experienced the sheer, heart-stopping wonder of seeing horse and rider move as one. The chestnut was silhouetted against the setting sun, his mane and tail streaming in the breeze, Jordan seeming more a part of the animal he rode than a separate entity, every movement fluid and supple, with a symmetry and grace that left her speechless with delight. From the back of her mind came the remembrance that Jordan's star-sign was Sagittarius, the archer, often portrayed as a centaur, half-man, half-horse, and the image seemed particularly fitting now.

'Bloody hell!' There was awe in the voice of the groom behind her. 'And to think he hasn't been on a horse in months!'

But threading through the admiration was a note of anxiety that mirrored the concern Michael made no attempt to conceal on his own face and that jarred painfully, destroying her delight with the realisation that this was the first time Jordan had ridden since his accident— and that it had been because of her that Jordan had come out with them at all. Her initial relief and joy at the fact that he had not lost his nerve completely ebbed away before a wave of concern at the thought of the possible consequences of this unexpected development.

But when Jordan finally brought Flame to a halt beside the waiting group, he avoided both her anxious eyes and his brother's as he silently reached for the leading-rein once more. His horse was lathered with sweat, and dark patches stained Jordan's shirt, clear evidence of the physical test to which he had subjected himself, but his face was firmly closed against any attempt to gauge his feelings. *Not a word,* his expression seemed to say. *Don't say a word!* And when Michael seemed about to speak, it was Madeleine who laid a warning hand on his arm to silence him.

When they arrived back at the stables, the ordered routine of unsaddling, feeding and settling the horses for the night meant that no one had time to talk on any subject other than practical matters for quite some time. Madeleine was drawn into the bustle too as, with the help of one of the grooms, she learned a few basic facts about stable management, discovering in the process that Dove was a gentle, placid creature who bore her unpractised fumblings with gentle patience, making her wonder how she could ever have been afraid of her before. Jordan appeared in the doorway just as she was giving the grey mare a last, affectionate pat.

'Everything OK?' he asked, his voice easy and light. If he felt any strain he hid it well, though he couldn't conceal the tightness of the muscles of his face, the greyish tinge to his skin, so that Madeleine had to struggle with the urge to put her arms around him, ease that too taut stance and smooth the harsh lines from his face. She knew Jordan would never let her close enough for that. 'So what did you think of your first ride?'

'I think I could get to like it,' Madeleine said honestly, and a tiny ray of warmth eased the cold stillness of Jordan's expression.

'You're welcome to have another try, any time you like. Dove would probably enjoy the exercise.' The warmth in his tone spread into what was almost a smile, as Madeleine smoothed Dove's grey neck. 'You've got more confidence already.'

'She's so gentle.' Madeleine's voice was uneven. She was painfully aware of the fact that the approval in Jordan's voice was for her interest in the horses he so valued, but at least it was a beginning, a tiny breakthrough into the reserve he'd imposed between them. 'And she's really quite small—not like that great chestnut beast of yours. I wouldn't like to try to ride him, especially not the first time after——'

She broke off abruptly as something slid down over Jordan's face, closing it against her.

'Peter again, I suppose?' he drawled sardonically, his tone making Madeleine rush on unguardedly.

'I don't know how you could—weren't you afraid?'

'Afraid?' Jordan looked stunned, as if fear had never entered into it. 'Not of Flame,' he added obscurely. 'I know him—I trust him.'

Trust. Coming so soon after his declaration that he couldn't trust her, the word stung bitterly and Madeleine could have wept at the sight of the suspicion that once again darkened those light grey eyes.

'"A four-legged friend, a four-legged friend",' she sang with bitter satire.

'"He'll never let you down",' Jordan finished sharply. 'Exactly.'

She'd lost him again, Madeleine reflected miserably. From the moment Peter's name had entered the conversation, all trace of warmth had faded from Jordan's face, leaving it bleak and coldly hostile. Perhaps there was a way to win him round again—if she wanted to take it—but did she? Wouldn't that be laying herself open to the sort of callousness he had shown to Sukey?

For a long moment common sense warred with a deeper, more primitive need, but in the end that need won which, if Madeleine was honest, she had always known it would. She could not stay away from Jordan, that was why she had come here today though she knew it would have been safer to stay away; safer, but sterile. Those moments in Jordan's arms, his kisses and the emotions they had aroused in her had taught her that, right now, Jordan was what she needed. She didn't know what the future might bring, but she would leave that to take care of itself. For the present she needed to be with him, see him, talk to him, and she would take any chance that would allow her to do that.

'If you meant what you said about teaching me to ride,' she blurted out impetuously, 'I'd like to take you up on it.' She *did* want to learn to ride, she rationalised to herself. The brief experience of being on Dove's back had been surprisingly enjoyable, something she wanted to repeat. She watched Jordan's face anxiously, waiting for his response with every nerve stretched tight with tension. If he refused she would have no second chance.

'Any time.' Jordan's reply came so easily that for a second she could hardly believe she had heard correctly. 'We could start tomorrow, if you like.'

If she liked! Madeleine's heart soared, the prospect of seeing him the following day lightening the dissatisfaction and unease she felt at having to leave like this, with nothing resolved between them. But when she was in her car, driving down the country lanes towards her home, she had time to think, to consider Jordan's reaction more realistically. With Peter's words once more sounding in her ears, she was forced to admit that things had not been as easy as they had seemed. It had been her interest in the horses that Jordan had welcomed, horses and riding, around which his world centred so strongly that she doubted if anything else would ever touch him. If she hadn't shown an interest in that world, would he ever have invited her back to Northcote simply for herself? With an aching heart Madeleine acknowledged that she doubted that he would.

Her feelings on that matter were reinforced by the experience of her first riding lesson the next day, and all the other lessons that followed from it. Jordan was always polite, always calm and patient, a perfect teacher, but that was all. He kept his distance mentally as well as physically, until Madeleine was forced to wonder if she had dreamed that kiss on the afternoon of her first visit to Northcote. On one level his behaviour couldn't be faulted, but on another she found herself wishing that he would show some emotion—*any* emotion. She almost felt that the violent anger he had shown on the journey back to the Manor would be preferable, at least then she would have something to react to.

She often returned home from Northcote feeling very low and intensely frustrated. Being with Jordan and yet getting nothing from him but the polite friendliness he showed to anyone, the grooms who worked for him, for example, was almost more painful than never seeing him at all, and she didn't like the way it made her feel. It was as if she was some gauche adolescent, struck stupid by an overwhelming crush on an attractive man, but unable to put her feelings into words, reduced to tagging along beside him as she and her sisters had once trailed after boys in their early teenage years when they had first become aware of the attractions of the opposite sex.

At such times she came close to deciding to stop the lessons altogether; she was only tormenting herself by being so physically close to Jordan and yet knowing that mentally they were still miles apart. Once she even picked up the telephone to ring Jordan and tell him she would not be going to Northcote that evening, but half-way through dialling his number her resolve weakened and her hand stilled.

She couldn't do it. Unsatisfactory as they were, these afternoons and evenings were all she had, and she couldn't bear to lose them. With a sigh of resignation she put the receiver down again. Perhaps she was deceiving herself, she didn't know, all she did know was that she had to keep trying. How long Jordan would keep up the lessons she couldn't guess—perhaps she would have a few months, perhaps less—but in that time she might just be able to build up some sort of relationship with Jordan and he might come to trust her as she so desperately needed him to.

Madeleine was at Northcote, her lesson for that afternoon just completed, when Rupert and Geraldine, accompanied by Peter, came to deliver an invitation to their wedding. Peter was clearly none too pleased to find Madeleine there, his handsome face marred by a sullen expression that made him look like a sulky small boy. The contributions he made to the conversation were so perfunctory as to be positively rude, and he spent most of the afternoon glowering in his chair, only coming alive when the talk inevitably turned to the local horse trials that were to be held the following month.

'Have you entered both your horses, Jordy?' he asked with careful casualness but, knowing what was behind the loaded words, Madeleine tensed instinctively. Jordan had often joined her on her rides, mounted on either Diamond or Flame, but such quiet treks were very different from the physical endurance of a cross-country trial and she knew from a remark that Michael had let slip that he had not taken part in the intensive, strenuous training that such events required.

'Flame and Diamond will both be competing,' Jordan answered quietly.

'Oh, lord!' Peter groaned in mock despair. 'That's it, then. I might just as well kiss the prize money goodbye right here and now if you're riding—and there's a lady I particularly wanted to impress——'

He broke off abruptly as Rupert's elegantly booted foot made painful contact with his ankle, the unsubtle warning heightening Madeleine's tension. She knew that Michael was to ride both horses, that Jordan had no plans to compete, and it was more than likely that Peter knew that, too.

'I hadn't planned to ride.' Jordan's tone was cold.

'Not ride!' Disbelief rang in Peter's voice. 'Jordy, you can't mean it! I was thinking of having a bet with you— nothing huge—just a few quid—highest placing wins. You've always beaten me before, you can't deny me my chance of revenge.'

Madeleine's mouth felt dry and she sat stiffly on the edge of her chair. Something in the way Peter had said 'revenge' had alerted her; she was sure he was baiting Jordan deliberately. A swift glance at the handsome face opposite her revealed the enjoyment gleaming in the bright blue eyes. Peter's jealousy was finally coming out into the open.

'Ask Michael.' Jordan's voice had an edge to it now.

'Michael's no good!' Peter exclaimed, ignoring the furious glances his brother was giving him. 'No offence to Mick, but you're the star—the local celebrity. The organisers have been selling tickets on your name alone— you can't chicken out now.'

The last words dropped into a silence that could have been cut with a knife, the insulting implication of cowardice impossible to ignore. Madeleine's eyes went to Jordan's face, seeing his tension in the way he sat, the lines etched on to his face. For a second those silver eyes met hers, but almost immediately the heavy lids dropped over them again, hiding their expression from her.

'Maddy,' Peter appealed to her, 'persuade him to change his mind. He'll——' He broke off as Madeleine froze him with a flash of her blue eyes.

'It's Jordan's decision, Peter,' she said firmly. 'No one else's.'

She was thankful that Peter would never know the struggle it had cost her to keep her voice calm and strong. His assumption that she had any influence with Jordan had stung painfully, the stab of bitterness increased by Jordan's deliberate lowering of his eyes, cutting her out. His eyes had lifted again now, she could feel his gaze on her face, her cheek burning where it rested.

'I think it's time we were going.' Rupert was getting to his feet in evident embarrassment. Madeleine half rose, too, then stilled as Jordan's voice suddenly broke into the awkward silence.

'You're on, Peter,' he said clearly. 'I'll ride Diamond.'

No! Madeleine wanted to cry as the two men shook hands on the bet. Don't do it! But she knew Jordan would never listen to her. If she had had any foolish hopes on that matter, his deliberate withdrawal had killed them once and for all. There was a sour taste in her mouth as she looked into Peter's face and saw it fill with a mixture of astonishment and a hateful, gloating triumph.

'Why don't you stay for dinner?' It was Michael who made the suggestion. He had emerged from the stables as soon as the Evensleighs' car had disappeared down the drive, appearing so promptly that Madeleine suspected him of deliberately avoiding their visitors.

Hesitantly, she turned to Jordan to discover his reaction to his brother's suggestion and, to her surprise and delight, found that he was nodding agreement.

'Why not?' he said offhandedly. 'There's more than enough for three, and if I remember rightly I still owe you that dinner I promised you.'

Madeleine needed no further urging. Perhaps it was foolish and naïve to pin her hopes on Jordan's belated remembrance of his promise—made a lifetime ago, it seemed—but she was past caring, snatching gratefully at the tiny crumb of friendship he had flung her way. Some deep inner instinct told her that tonight would be special, make or break as far as she and Jordan were concerned, and she had no intention of missing out on even the tiniest opportunity.

A less sensitive observer watching the three of them over the dinner table that night might have concluded that Jordan's decision to ride in the horse trials had affected him very little, but Madeleine was intensely aware of the small signs that betrayed his inner disquiet. Aided by Michael he maintained a flow of casual conversation with apparent ease, but the bleak, opaque look in his eyes, a tautness about the muscles of his mouth and jaw revealed that his mind was very much on other things. There was an unnatural precision about every movement of his hands too, as if he feared that some tremor might betray his composure for the act Madeleine was convinced it was. She was sure that Michael, too, had noted that his brother was drinking steadily, if undramatically, though without an apparent effect; he remained as controlled and restrained as ever.

Just after eleven Michael excused himself and retired to bed. Madeleine lingered a while in the hope that Jordan might say something that would give her an opening into a discussion of the worries that had nagged at her mind ever since Peter's taunting challenge, but he kept firmly to neutral topics and when the conversation became desultory she had no option but to decide that it was time for her to leave.

As she turned the key in the Mini's ignition the engine coughed, spluttered, and died. With an exclamation of annoyance she tried again, with no better result.

'Oh, blast the thing! I thought I'd got this problem sorted out!'

Her irritation fled as, glancing at Jordan through the car window, she saw his face in the moonlight, the eerie glow casting shadows across it, throwing into sharp relief the lines of stress, etching them more deeply than before. In that second she sensed his tension and, recalling her earlier conviction that this evening would be somehow important, every instinct she possessed cried out to her not to go, not to give him time to rebuild his defences against her as he had done before. Something hung on the air, dark and ominous like the heaviness before a storm. Her decision was taken and acted on before she had time to consider whether it was a wise or safe move to make.

'If I try any more I'll flood the wretched thing,' she declared for Jordan's benefit, and proceeded to do just that, the engine dying on a rasping shudder. 'Well, that's that! She'll not get me home tonight.'

With an acting ability that surprised herself, she got out of the car and slammed the door in exasperated annoyance.

'Just what am I supposed to do now?'

'I'll drive you back,' Jordan offered, but that was not at all what Madeleine had in mind.

'Oh, no, you don't—not after what you had to drink at dinner. Besides, you don't know the roads—it's too much of a risk. I'll have to stay here.'

'None of the rooms are finished yet,' Jordan protested, the fact that he so clearly didn't want her to stay simply reinforcing her determination to do just that.

'Roughing it for one night won't hurt me—and I know you have a spare bed. I haven't any nightclothes, though,' she added in an attempt to lighten an atmosphere that had become noticeably cooler. 'You'll have to lend me some pyjamas.'

'I don't wear the things!' Driven into a corner, Jordan showed no awareness of the intimacy of the personal detail he had inadvertently revealed. Every taut muscle in his body, his very stance declared his hostility to Madeleine's suggestion, his grey eyes blazing with such cold anger that she had to nerve herself to go on.

'Well, a shirt will do.' She was proud of the insouciance of her tone, though it cost her a struggle to keep her voice even, her stomach clenching painfully as she met the full force of those steely grey eyes. If he found one more reason for her not to stay, she doubted if she would have the courage to stand up to him any more.

'You'll have to ring your mother.' The concession came harshly, grudgingly, and it was only as her breath escaped in a sigh of relief that Madeleine became aware of the way she had been holding it in as she waited for his reply.

'Yes, I will. Can I use your phone?'

But she was talking to the empty air, for Jordan had already turned on his heel and stalked back into the house. Taking a deep breath and squaring her shoulders determinedly, Madeleine followed him inside.

CHAPTER ELEVEN

MADELEINE was never sure what had woken her, only aware of the fact that some sound had penetrated the uneasy doze into which she had fallen after lying awake for what seemed like an age. She stirred restlessly, opening blurred eyes to stare with a complete lack of recognition at the unfamiliar room in the grey half-light. She felt hot and sticky, the shirt she wore instead of a nightdress damp with sweat—Jordan's shirt, she remembered belatedly—and this was Jordan's room. He had escorted her here as soon as she had finished the telephone call to her mother, his body stiff with unspoken hostility, his mouth drawn into a thin, hard line. With a sighing groan, Madeleine recalled how he had flung the shirt down on the bed and departed with only a curt 'goodnight', leaving her to undress and get into bed in a mood of total despondency.

So much for her hopes that if she stayed she might finally find a way of getting through to him! Jordan couldn't have made it more obvious that her presence was unwelcome, and she was as far away from him in this room as she would have been if she'd gone home. It had all been a terrible mistake and, by her insistence on staying, she had probably destroyed even the fragile, tenuous links there had been between them before. Miserably Madeleine punched her pillows into a softer shape, expressing her feelings in the unnecessary force with which she pummelled them, and lay back, trying to compose her mind so that she had some hope of sleep.

She was still lying stiffly, staring blankly at the ceiling, when she heard the sound again.

At once she sat up hastily, every nerve alive, straining her ears to catch it again. Nothing. But she *had* heard it, the noise of a door opening and closing somewhere below on the ground floor. Burglars?

Idiot! she reproved herself. It was probably just Jordan or Michael—but a glance at her watch told her that it was barely two in the morning, not the sort of time for anyone to be still awake. Another sound from the room directly underneath hers had her sitting up hastily, swinging her legs out of the bed. It was no good, she had no chance of sleep at all unless she investigated.

Keeping close to the wall, and moving as quietly as possible, she crept downstairs, her heart thudding painfully. A thin strip of light showed underneath the door into the living-room and at the sight of it Madeleine's tension eased slightly. Not burglars then, but just who was still up and awake at this time? Tentatively she pushed open the door. A fire burned in the grate, its glowing warmth welcome on a chilly night, but there was no such welcome on the face of the man who stood before it.

'Jordan!' Relief, shock and uncertainty combined to make Madeleine's voice high and sharp.

'What the hell are you doing here?' It was an angry snarl, Jordan's eyes as cold and bleak as a November sky. 'I thought you were asleep hours ago.'

'I—I heard a noise. I thought it might be burglars.'

'Well, now you know it wasn't. So you can just go back to bed.'

'Oh, but——' Why was he still up, fully dressed and not thinking of sleep for some time yet, if the steaming pot of coffee on the table was anything to go by?

'Oh, but nothing,' Jordan cut in, his tone as harsh and unyielding as his face. 'I appreciate your concern,' he continued in a voice that made nonsense of the polite words, 'but as you can see there is nothing for you to worry about, so I would be grateful if you would just take yourself off upstairs and leave me alone.'

It was the last thing she wanted to do. She desperately wanted to know what worries had kept him awake, her thoughts going back to Peter's challenge, the strain that had shown on Jordan's face throughout the rest of the evening, but meeting that icy gaze she knew she had no alternative but to do just as he said. She was unable to control the shiver that shook her, as if Jordan's cold glance had had a physical effect. Suddenly and unexpectedly Jordan's expression changed.

'You're cold!' he said, a note of concern in his voice, and Madeleine seized on the opportunity his momentary softening offered her.

'I'm frozen,' she declared in a voice that shook very slightly. 'If I could just sit by the fire for a moment——'

She was moving forward as she spoke, and Jordan made no move to stop her, though his lips tightened perceptibly as if holding back some angry rejection of her action. For a moment he hesitated then, with a shrug that indicated resigned acceptance, he picked up a grey quilted jacket that lay on the settee and slung it round her shoulders.

'This should warm you up,' he said gruffly. 'And perhaps you'd like some coffee?'

'That would be lovely.' Madeleine sank into a chair, her legs feeling like cotton wool underneath her. He was going to let her stay, for a while, at least. What she did with that time was up to her.

She accepted the cup Jordan handed her, with a smile of thanks, and she sipped at its contents, huddling further into Jordan's jacket. Its warmth was comforting, it smelt faintly of Jordan and the musky scent of horses and— she froze suddenly. The outside of the jacket was slightly damp, still with the tang of night air clinging to it, and now that she looked closely she saw that Jordan's hair, too, was darkened by a misting of fine raindrops. Not only was he still wide awake at this God-forsaken hour, but he had evidently been out and had only just returned.

Jordan moved to the chair opposite, settling himself in it and stretching his legs out in front of him. His movements had a stiff awkwardness that spoke of intense physical tiredness, reminding her of the time in her home when they had returned from their first visit to Northcote, and her concern for him was strong enough to overcome her hesitancy over speaking again.

'Is your leg very bad?' she blurted out hastily. 'Is that why you couldn't sleep?'

'Partly.' The guarded tone gave nothing away. 'Look, I'm sorry if I was a bit abrupt, but I had the fright of my life when the door opened and you came in looking——'

He broke off sharply, but the swift flicker of a glance down from her face brought a wash of colour to Madeleine's cheeks as she remembered belatedly that she was wearing nothing but the pale blue shirt Jordan had lent her to wear as a nightdress.

Suddenly she saw herself as he must be seeing her, dark hair tumbling in soft disarray around a pale face in which her blue eyes were wide and bright with tension. The top two buttons of the shirt were open to reveal the graceful line of her throat, long slender legs showed beneath the blue cotton that barely covered her thighs, and the soft material clung to every curve when she moved.

Suddenly Jordan lifted his eyes and his silver gaze held hers. For an electric moment everything else became unimportant, nothing mattered beyond the fact that Jordan was a devastatingly attractive man, one who drew her to him more with every meeting, and, from the gleam in those light eyes, a man who was equally aware of her as a woman. A primitive yearning for physical contact, a longing to be beside him, not sitting with several yards of carpet between them, lit up inside Madeleine, making her head swim with its intensity and with the shock of realisation that she had almost moved, and almost gone to his chair...

Jordan's eyes dropped to his coffee with an abruptness that jolted her back to reality with a savage sense of shock, but she had no time to let his action get through to her because, like a lightning flash illuminating a darkened landscape, it suddenly came to her that *this* was the opportunity she had been waiting for. Right here and now was the moment she had known had to come, the reason she had had to stay.

'Tell me what's wrong, Jordan. Is it something about Sukey?' she said softly and sensed the burning wave of hostile rejection of her words that emanated from him, even though he hadn't moved a muscle and was still not looking at her. From somewhere deep inside herself she dragged up the courage to go on. 'Jordan, please listen to me! Don't block me out like this—I want to help.'

His silence seemed to last for ever. She could almost feel his mental conflict as if it were her own, the arguments for and against being weighed on the scales of his mind, and she knew she had to take a risk to win him round.

'I know you don't want to talk about your accident.' With a determined effort she kept her voice and expression calm and neutral, though it was harder than anything she'd ever done. Her control almost broke when she saw his head go back as if she'd struck him, his breath hissing between his teeth. It took all her strength to press home her advantage. 'You've been blocking that off for too long, trying to pretend it never happened—but it did!'

Madeleine paused, hoping for some response, but none came. Jordan's narrowed eyes were watchful and wary, like those of a hunted animal, and when he made a move as if to get out of his seat she knew she had to change her tactics or lose him completely.

'Jordan, please—you helped me by listening to my memories of my father; I only want to do the same for you.'

She held her breath, waiting. His nod when it came at last was barely perceptible, but it was there and he had settled back in his chair, heavily hooded grey eyes watching her with such a burning intensity that she felt her skin might actually be scorched where they had rested.

'Say what you have to stay,' he commanded harshly.

Madeleine drew a long, uneven breath. She wasn't at all sure she was winning, but at least she hadn't lost completely.

'Do you remember the day we first went to Northcote—how you told me that the unhappy memories of your past can pile up in your mind? You compared it to the soiled bedding in a horse's stall, and you said the only way to stop them fouling up your life was to clear them out of the way once and for all.'

She forced herself to look straight into those watchful grey eyes, wetting dry lips nervously with her tongue before she could continue.

'That's what you've been doing with your memories of your accident, not letting them out, and they're eating you up inside. You have to tell someone, Jordan, or it will destroy you!'

A blank, worrying silence descended when she had finished speaking, but Madeleine knew she could not be the one to break it. That move had to come from Jordan, and she could only sit tensely in her seat and pray that he would decide to make it. The silence lengthened, stretching her nerves tighter with every second until she was almost at screaming pitch then, just as she thought she could wait no longer, that she had failed, Jordan stirred restlessly, pushing one hand through the thick crispness of his hair.

'Peter told you about Sukey,' he said slowly, and the dull, flat tone of his voice tore at Madeleine's heart.

'He told me what he knew,' she said carefully.

'You didn't believe him?' Jordan's question came curtly, almost angrily, but Madeleine was too set on her course to let his attitude deter her now.

'We both know Peter.' Her voice was low but firm. 'He only hears what he wants to hear—look at the way he kept on at me about that wretched Ball. I'd take anything he said with more than a pinch of salt.'

Almost anything, an unhappy little voice in her mind added. She couldn't deny the truth of Peter's statement that Jordan cared more for his horses than he did anyone else. Resolutely Madeleine pushed that thought away and concentrated her attention on Jordan. Was she imagining things, or had there been the slightest hint of relaxation of the tension in Jordan's shoulder muscles? One swift glance at his eyes told her that he had come to his decision and she almost stopped breathing as she waited for him to speak.

'I met Sukey two years ago.' Jordan's voice was flat and lifeless, he might have been talking about the weather or the price of fish. 'She was seventeen then, bright, lively and very, very pretty.'

A sadly reminiscent smile curled his lips for a moment but was ruthlessly suppressed, driven away by a bitterness that made Madeleine flinch inwardly.

'I was captivated by her. She was—is—a delightful creature, tiny and fragile, like a little bird, with dark hair, big brown eyes and a vivacious character. She was no virgin, but I knew that—what I didn't know was that she had a history of instability, starting way back in her childhood. After a time she became very demanding, always wanting to know where I was, what I was doing, who I was with. She resented the time I had to spend working with the horses, and she'd fly into a jealous rage if I so much as *looked* at another woman. One time, when she thought I'd been paying too much attention to one of the girl grooms, she actually attacked her—scratched her face, pulled out handfuls of her hair.'

Jordan sighed and rubbed the back of his hand across his eyes in a gesture of weariness.

'What there was between us died after that—on my part, at least. I tried to be kind, told her we could still be friends, but she wouldn't let go. Wherever I went she was always there, hounding me. She got drunk, told everyone how appallingly I'd treated her, warned off any woman I showed an interest in. I tried to be patient—but then she started saying she was pregnant.'

Some movement or change of expression betrayed Madeleine. Jordan's eyes swung to her face, darkening at what he saw there.

'Peter swallowed that one,' he said bleakly. 'Madeleine, I don't know if Sukey *was* pregnant—I only know that if she was, it couldn't have been my child. I hadn't slept with her for over six months—that was the first thing that died between us—and she was claiming to be just six weeks pregnant.'

Use your intuition, her mother had said, and that instinct was telling her that Jordan spoke the truth, so she simply nodded silently and waited for him to continue.

'Sukey told everyone the baby was mine. She insisted that I should marry her. She even managed to get herself into the competitors' enclosure at the Horse of the Year Show when Michael was competing, and threw a hysterical scene.' Jordan stared at a patch of carpet just inches away from his feet. 'I'm not proud of the way I behaved then. I was sick of her hounding me; I'd have done anything to get her off my back. But I should have been more gentle. If I'd known . . .'' His voice faded into silence.

'What happened?' Madeleine prompted softly and Jordan's eyes suddenly lifted to her face. What she saw there made her stiffen in shock. The emotion he had smoothed from his voice burned in their depths, making her draw in her breath sharply.

'You asked about the accident,' he said sardonically. 'Sukey caused it.'

It was impossible to control the involuntary start of reaction, and a twisted smile flickered across Jordan's face.

'You were right when you said I'd been blocking off what had happened. I didn't want to admit that I was finished, that Sukey had ruined my career.'

I was finished. Three simple words in a voice as hard as stone, but behind that expressionless statement burned a raw intensity that said more about the way Jordan was feeling than a thousand sentences could ever do. For a moment Madeleine thought he was going to stop there, but she knew there was more to be said, things that still had to be cleared from her mind. Acting instinctively, she leaned forward and laid her hand on his arm.

'The accident, Jordan,' she said softly, drawing on the few details she knew, pushing him as hard as she dared. 'You were riding, training Swallow, in the field by your home——'

'I wanted Swallow really fit for the Olympic trials,' Jordan's voice took up the story. 'I knew she was championship material. I'd set up a course of jumps, there was one—a triple—which was particularly difficult, it had an awkward turn just before you got to it. Swallow was very fast—I don't know where she came from——'

It took Madeleine a second to realise that 'she' was not the horse, but Sukey.

'One minute there was no one there, the next Sukey had run out into the field, right in our path.'

The room seemed to blur around Madeleine as she imagined what had happened, the horse rearing up, falling, shattering her own leg and trapping Jordan under the weight of her body—and Sukey? Without being aware that she had spoken she found she had asked the question out loud. Jordan's face twisted savagely.

'She was completely unhurt. I don't know how we managed to miss her, but the last thing I remember was seeing her running away.'

'Why did you never tell anyone what she'd done?'

Jordan sighed wearily, pushing both his hands through his hair. 'I don't think she meant to hurt me, I think she meant to injure Swallow; she'd always said I cared more for the horses than I did for her. And I felt—responsible. If I hadn't rejected her so publicly she'd never have done it. I also thought that if I kept quiet she'd see that I didn't want to hurt her, and then perhaps she'd leave me alone.'

'And now?'

'Now?' Jordan repeated bleakly. 'I don't know. Sukey left me alone while I was in hospital—and for a time after I came out. She'd always revelled in my success, the reflected glory of being my girlfriend was part of what drew her to me, so I suppose someone who couldn't ride—couldn't even walk—held no attraction for her. I heard she found another man for a while, but that broke up and suddenly she was back. I'd had plenty of time to think while I was laid up, and I'd already decided on a move. Mick and I have had plans for these stables for a long time, but I suppose I thought that by coming north I'd escape from Sukey, too. But then, at Badminton, I saw Sukey again. She said she knew where I was and she'd follow me wherever I went.'

Peter had told Sukey where Jordan lived—and he had offered her somewhere to stay, too! Suddenly Madeleine recalled Peter's remark about a girl he particularly wanted to impress.

'Peter——' she began but Jordan was there before her.

'He's invited Sukey to the horse trials. Angela, Mick's wife, found that out. She rang me this morning.'

'Surely, after all this time——' Madeleine stopped, silenced by the look on Jordan's face. 'Do you hate her very much?' she asked hesitantly.

'Hate?' Jordan echoed the word consideringly. 'No. Originally I felt sorry for her, but then she started on this private vendetta—damn it, Madeleine! Swallow died because of that silly little bitch.'

She should have expected that. *This* was what he couldn't forgive, Swallow's death and the destruction of his own career.

'It was the kindest thing—she'd broken her leg.'

'So did I!' Jordan's bitterness lashed her. 'They didn't shoot me, though God knows there were times in that hospital when I wished they had! And still Sukey won't let go!'

'She thinks she loves you.'

'Love!' Jordan's laugh was an ugly sound, his voice thick with black cynicism. 'You can't call that perverted possessiveness *love*!'

For the first time since he had started to talk, Madeleine sensed those steel doors in Jordan's mind slam shut against her, but now she thought she understood why he was so determined to shut her out. Sukey's twisted sort of love had scarred Jordan mentally as well as physically, and he had no intention of letting anyone get close ever again. If he left no room for feeling, then he left no room for hurt, either.

'Not everyone's love gets distorted like Sukey's. Someone else——'

'I don't want anyone else!' Jordan got to his feet with a violent movement that jarred his leg, making Madeleine grit her teeth against a cry of concern. 'Do you think I'd lay myself open to that again? I'll stick to horses—you can trust them.'

A four-legged friend ... The song came back to haunt her, its words having a sharper, cutting edge because now she knew.

She had acknowledged on the night of the Ball that Jordan was the sort of man she could fall in love with, had admitted to herself that perhaps she was already part-way along the road that led her to caring for him more than for any person in her life before. But her assessment of her own reaction had been desperately inaccurate. She wasn't part-way to anything; she was already there.

She loved Jordan. Perhaps, in a way, she had loved him before she had even known it, giving her heart in the first moment she had seen him. She had been so drawn to him, forming a bond that went beyond the everyday boundaries of words and gestures, reaching right to the very core of her being.

But how could she convince him of what she felt, when his mind was so closed against her, against anyone? One thing she knew, she couldn't even try to tell him tonight. The dark memories were too near the surface for him to tolerate that. Frantically she hunted for something to say, anything that would distract her from those all-important words, 'I love you,' that seemed to burn on her tongue, so that she was afraid she might blurt them out without thinking.

'But perhaps your career isn't finished. You can still ride—the doctor said——' The look on Jordan's face stopped her dead, a chill shivering down her spine.

'I know what the doctor said—but he was talking about my leg. In time, that might become almost as strong as before, I don't know, but I do know one thing—I can't forget what happened, and tonight proved that.'

'Tonight?' His jacket had been damp—and his hair—
'You went out! You were riding—at this time of night!'

Jordan nodded, his mouth tightening grimly. 'There's
a full moon, it's almost as clear as day, I've ridden in
worse conditions.'

'But why?'

'After the accident, when I started to recover, I
couldn't get on a horse without seeing Sukey. All the
pleasure went out of riding—I couldn't do it—until that
day when Mick suggested you rode.'

That day when he had forced himself to ride for *her*
sake. It was a tiny thing, but it was enough to sustain a
glimmer of hope.

'Tonight, when you'd gone to bed, I couldn't sleep.
I'd accepted Peter's challenge, but I didn't know if I
could do it, if I could even take a horse over a jump.
So I saddled Diamond and took her out——' Jordan's
hand twisted together, his knuckles showing white. 'It
took me half an hour, but I did it——But,' he went on,
cutting into Madeleine's exclamation of delight, 'every
time I face a jump I see Sukey running towards me.'
Roughly, he pushed his hands through the thickness of
his hair. 'I don't know if I'll ever be free of her, especially not when she's coming to the trials.'

Jordan's tone and the thought of the possible repercussions that might result from Sukey's arrival in Holtby
made Madeleine shiver fearfully. There had to be something they could do! If she was Sukey, what would convince her that she had lost Jordan for good? Another
girlfriend? No, it needed more than that. A faint spark
of an idea lit in her mind.

'What if you were engaged to someone else? If Sukey
thought you were going to be married, would she get
the message then and leave you alone?'

Jordan's grey eyes met her blue ones, and she saw a gleam of hope in them. 'It might just work. But where the hell am I to find——'

'Right here,' Madeleine interrupted, stopping him dead. 'Jordan, it doesn't have to be real,' she rushed on, trying to silence her own heart as it cried out against a pretence of what she now knew she wanted more than anything in the world. 'We're friends——' That hurt, making her catch her breath sharply. 'I've no commitments and I know about Sukey. She can try all the tricks she likes, but she won't worry me. We can claim to be engaged for three months—six—as long as it takes to convince her and then——' She couldn't say it, couldn't contemplate what would happen then, let alone put it into words. They caught in her throat, choking her, but Jordan didn't seem to notice her abrupt silence.

'You'd do that?' he asked incredulously.

'I told you—we're friends.' Perhaps if she repeated the word often enough she would come to accept it, to believe that that was all he was to her.

'I couldn't ask——'

'You didn't.' She had her voice under control now. It sounded firm, even confident. 'I offered.'

Say yes, Jordan! she begged him silently. Please say yes! But this had to be *his* decision, his alone.

'It might just work,' Jordan said slowly, and she caught the note of acceptance in his voice.

'That's settled, then,' she declared brightly, not giving him time to reconsider. 'As from now, we're engaged.' She hesitated, but couldn't resist the impulse to add, 'So, as your fiancée, do I get a kiss?'

Fool! she reproved herself fiercely, expecting to see Jordan's face close against her as her unguarded words drove him back in on himself. What did you have to say that for? But surprisingly Jordan smiled and, reaching out a hand, pulled her to her feet.

She didn't know which would be worse, the controlled restraint that showed how little he wanted this closeness, or the burning passion that had broken through those rigid barriers on such rare occasions before. Both would hurt bitterly, because they declared without words how wide the gulf was that still yawned between them.

But Jordan's kiss was light, almost brotherly, and warmed with a gentle affection. And, although the ache of longing and the searing need that burned deep inside her were far from sisterly, it was a beginning, and with that she had to be content.

Perhaps she would have the six months she had mentioned, perhaps less, but in that time she might just be able to heal the scars left by Sukey's actions. And then she might be able to show Jordan that there were other, gentler forms of love.

CHAPTER TWELVE

MADELEINE lay in bed in the room that had come to be considered hers whenever she stayed overnight at Northcote, a long way from sleep, in spite of the fact that it was very late. Her mind was straying over the events of the past few weeks, deliberately thinking of anything other than the fact that tomorrow was the day of the horse trials, the day when she would discover whether her plan to dissuade Sukey from any further action had worked or not.

She and Jordan had announced their 'engagement' the morning after they had agreed on it, Mick being the first to know, and his delight had set the pattern for everyone else's reaction. No one seemed to suspect that it was anything other than the true romance it appeared to be and, for Madeleine at least, it was only too easy to play the part of the loving fiancée in public. It was far harder to switch to the casual, uncommitted friend Jordan wanted her to be in private, to forget the allowances he made, the freedom he gave her to smile or touch or sometimes even to kiss him when someone else was in the room.

Jordan had insisted on buying her a ring, a symbol which Madeleine had tried to refuse, but he had squashed her protests with the irrefutable argument that they would never convince Sukey that their engagement was real if they didn't follow the traditions exactly. So, at a party held to celebrate her twenty-fifth birthday, Madeleine let him put the ring on her finger, although each time she looked at it the gleam of the stones seemed to stab at her with the reminder that none of this was real and it would very soon be over.

It was at her party that she had met Michael's wife Angela and his two small sons, who had arrived at Northcote that weekend. She took to them as swiftly as they did to her, their presence enhancing the pleasure of staying at the Hall as she did every weekend, sharing in the work of the stables and, under Jordan's careful guidance, continuing her riding lessons on the elderly Dove, whom she had now learned to handle fairly competently. Jordan often rode with her, mounted on either Flame or Diamond, and Madeleine treasured those quiet times together, the moments she spent in Jordan's company becoming more precious with every day that passed.

In the darkness, Madeleine sighed and stirred restlessly, her mind slipping away from her carefully imposed control and veering on to the subject of the coming horse trials. She had no idea how Jordan was feeling about tomorrow. She knew that he had trained hard during the past weeks, driving himself relentlessly, but never once had he shared with her his hopes or fears. Since the night he had opened up to her, telling her the truth about Sukey and his accident, that subject had been a closed book and, on that topic at least, he had been as withdrawn and distant as ever.

A sudden sound in the corridor drew Madeleine's attention, her head jerking round in shock as the door to her bedroom opened quietly. The light from the corridor outside shone on to a strong, masculine figure framed in the doorway.

'Jordan!' She sat up hastily, her heart pounding with apprehension at his sudden and unexpected appearance.

He had clearly prepared for bed, a navy towelling robe apparently his only clothing, his brown hair slightly ruffled, and after one glance at his face she knew what had kept him awake.

'Couldn't you sleep?' She kept her voice light with an effort, struggling not to let him see how affected she was by the shadows under his eyes, the lines of strain around his nose and mouth.

Jordan shook his head silently, then pushed a hand through his hair, the movement opening the front of his loosely belted robe over his powerfully made chest and shoulders, and, watching the muscles slide under his skin, Madeleine was overwhelmed with a longing to know the strength of those arms around her, feel them hold her close... She caught herself up sharply and patted the bed beside her, indicating that Jordan should come and sit down. Still without a word, he obeyed her.

'We could have a midnight feast,' she suggested teasingly, struggling to keep her thoughts away from the dangerous path they had been following. 'How do you fancy——'

'I shouldn't be here, Madeleine,' Jordan broke in suddenly, his grey eyes flashing in the moonlight. 'Someone might have seen me come in.'

'What if they did? We're engaged, aren't we?'

'We both know that means nothing,' Jordan declared harshly.

Pain tore at Madeleine, and she closed her hands on the cream cotton of the bedspread, her eyes fixed on the crumpled material.

'Does it?' she whispered softly.

Jordan froze for a second, his whole body absolutely still, but not before she had seen the tiny, convulsive movement that clenched his left hand.

'We're just friends,' he said stiffly.

'*Friends!*' How she had come to hate that word. 'Is that all, Jordan?'

Madeleine lifted her head as she spoke, looking straight into his eyes, frightening herself with the shock of the raw emotion she saw there, just for a moment, before his eyelids dropped for a second and he drew a long, unsteady breath. When he opened his eyes again they were as blank and indifferent as stone.

'What else could we be?' he asked coldly, the force of his rejection stunning her like a blow to her face.

'Don't do that to me!' she cried unhappily. Her mind felt bruised, hurting from the calculation with which he had deliberately withdrawn from her, and she didn't care if she gave herself away once and for all. 'Don't shut me out like that!'

Jordan's control wavered for a second, then slammed back into place. 'I think it's better this way.' The flat, lifeless tone tore through her mind like a scream. 'I should never have come—I'd better go and leave you in peace.'

Peace. It was a strange word to use when he was fighting her every step of the way. But the fact that he *was* fighting gave her some hope that there was some feeling there and that helped her find the words she needed.

'I don't want that peace if you don't share it—there is no peace in being shut off from you.'

'Madeleine!' Jordan groaned, his broad shoulders hunched despondently. He made a move as if to get up off the bed, but she reached out swiftly and caught at his arm, restraining him.

'Why did you come here tonight, Jordan?' she asked shakily.

'Because—because I need you.' The answer was torn from him, and Madeleine's heart twisted deep inside her.

'And I need you——' Her voice failed her as she saw the unspoken question in his eyes. 'I want you to hold me.' The words came out unevenly, breathlessly. 'Please, Jordan, just hold me.'

She didn't see him move because the ferocity of her own need blurred with his, multiplying it infinitely. She only knew she was in his arms and it was where she had always wanted to be, and that his kiss had swept away all barriers in a moment of longing and giving that blended them together as one.

Jordan's lips strayed from her mouth, across her cheek and into her hair, drifting featherlight kisses on its tumbled darkness, and her name was a crooning sound in his throat as he swung his legs up on to the bed, lying alongside her. With a soft sigh, Madeleine slid her arms around his neck to link her hands in the crisp hair at the base of his skull as her mouth sought his blindly.

Their lips met softly, gently, but as Madeleine would have increased the pressure of the kiss she felt the change in Jordan's mood, resistance stiffening his body. With a jolt, he lifted his head, the muscles in his neck tightening as he pulled against her restraining hands.

'Madeleine, no!' Jordan's voice was thick and rough.

'Yes,' Madeleine answered firmly, but he shook his head, the rough hairs that stubbled his chin scraping on the softness of her cheek.

'Stop this!' he ordered harshly, but she wasn't listening to his voice. His arms were still around her, his hands curving over her hips, and she could almost feel the conflict in his mind as his words said one thing, but his body another. With a small, wriggling movement she pulled the blankets from under him, hearing his swiftly indrawn breath as she slid up against the hard length of his body.

'Madeleine!' It was a warning, but one she was determined to ignore. She tried to press her lips to his again, but he wrenched his head away. 'I'm trying to protect you——'

'Are you?' Madeleine questioned sharply. 'Or are you really trying to protect yourself? It won't work, Jordan. You can't keep everything locked up inside—you'll destroy yourself.' Jordan's silence told her she had hit home. Drawing a long, shaky breath, she took a chance. 'I'm not Sukey.'

Jordan's groan was a sound of surrender as, with a rough movement, she was pulled close with a force that drove the breath from her body and her mouth was captured in a fierce kiss that crushed and bruised her lips beneath Jordan's. Madeleine shuddered, filled with a need so sharp it hurt. Whether he loved her or not didn't matter, all that mattered was this glorious release from the longing that had torn her in two.

After a long, mindless moment Jordan drew back slightly, taking her face between both his strong hands and searching her eyes, his own so very close that she felt that just for this moment he might be able to see into her thoughts as she looked back at him confidently, letting her love shine in her eyes for him to see.

'I want this,' she told him softly. 'I want it more than anything, but if you can look me straight in the face and tell me you don't—if it's truly not what you want——'

'Not what I want!' Jordan's laugh was shaken. 'Oh, God——'

'Then *say* it!'

'I want——' Jordan began then broke off and when he spoke again his voice was husky with emotion. 'I don't know how much I can give—I don't want you to be hurt.'

'Oh, Jordan,' Madeleine sighed. 'Can't you see, the thing that really hurts is when you shut me out.'

The silver eyes darkened swiftly before he closed them, and she felt the shudder of response that shook his body. After a long moment the heavy lids lifted again and she felt the pounding beat of her heart reverberate inside her head as she looked deep into his eyes.

'God, Madeleine,' he muttered hoarsely. 'Don't you know—I've never been able to shut you out, not from the very beginning.' His head lowered slowly towards her, his eyes never leaving her face. 'And I definitely can't do it now,' he whispered just before his lips came down hard on hers.

Their lovemaking was slow and sweet and infinitely tender. The emotions she had sensed in Jordan, once released, swept away all constraint so that, for this night at least, there were no steel walls, no barriers, only a mutual sharing so that for the first time they were as one, both needing, both wanting the same thing, and both giving equally to the other.

They slept, still tangled together, Jordan's arm tight around Madeleine's waist, her head pillowed on his chest, and when she stirred languorously in the morning, lifting heavy lids to smile her contentment straight into Jordan's watchful light eyes she saw there a peace that matched her own and knew that no shadows from the past had darkened his dreams as he lay beside her.

She was to remember that awakening with a pang of regret as the day wore on. From the moment Jordan left her bed and went to his own room to dress, the mood of the day changed and Jordan's with it. During the bustle of preparations, the grooming and loading of the horses into the horse-box, she barely caught a glimpse of him and, as he was to travel with Diamond while Madeleine joined Angela and her two sons in the car, it was some time before she actually spoke to him again. As soon as she did she knew that he had slipped away from her again, his replies curt and abstracted, his whole attention concentrated on the coming competition. Well, she could wait. Last night he had admitted that he needed her, and she hugged that fact to her like a small, secret warmth, sustaining her through the hours of waiting for the trials to be over so that Jordan could be with her again.

The dressage section of the competition passed off without a hitch, both Jordan and Michael earning high scores—as did Peter Evensleigh. But the real challenge, at least as far as Jordan was concerned, was yet to come. As the cross-country phase started, Madeleine and Angela positioned themselves part-way round the course, keeping a watchful eye on the two small boys to ensure that neither of them ran into the path of one of the competitors. Somewhere back at the start, Jordan and Michael waited for their turn to ride.

Jordan. Madeleine pictured him in her mind as she had last seen him. She had never been as affected by his physical attraction as she had today, seeing him for the first time, in the close-fitting black jacket and pale jodhpurs, beautifully polished high boots on his feet and an immaculate white cravat at his throat, and then in the fine silk shirt like a jockey's that he had changed into for the cross-country section. The light grey crossed with white picked up the smoky colour of his eyes, highlighting the tan he had acquired through weeks of outdoor training, and the soft silk clung to the firm lines of his chest and shoulders like a second skin, emphasising their honed strength with a devastating potency. The early summer sun had bleached his hair on top, giving it a striking two-tone effect, the darker brown showing only when a breeze lifted it. Recalling how Jordan had sprawled on the rug next to her while they ate a picnic lunch, Madeleine felt her heart thud unevenly.

'Not long now.' Angela's voice broke into her thoughts. 'That was number thirty-six. Mick's forty-one and Jordan fifty, so we should see them soon.'

Madeleine's smile of acknowledgement was half-hearted. She wanted this stage over. Peter had already ridden, pounding round the course on a huge bay, clearing the fences in a way that, according to Angela, owed more to his horse's strength than his own over-rated riding ability, and soon Jordan would follow him. Madeleine had no idea of their relative positions in the overall ratings, and she didn't want to know. The bet meant nothing to her. She just wanted Jordan to complete the course in safety.

'There's Daddy!' Angela cried and the children bounced excitedly on the grass, shouting encouragement as Michael and Flame cleared a wide ditch and swung away from them towards a fence made up of apparently randomly piled logs. When she had walked the four-mile course with Jordan earlier that morning, Madeleine had learned that all the fences had their own names: the Zigzag, the Quarry, the Ski-jump, and the ominously named Coffin, a terrifying-looking combination of a high, rustic fence and a narrow, water-filled ditch that had given her the shudders simply to look at it.

The sky had darkened threateningly by the time Madeleine heard Jordan's name and number announced

over the loudspeakers, and the first spots of rain were
beginning to fall as the slim, grey and white-clad figure
on the black horse cleared the ditch that Michael had
jumped a short time before. Behind her, Angela was
hurrying the boys into raincoats, but Madeleine stood
transfixed, her heart beating high up in her throat, willing
Jordan to feel her love and encouragement as Diamond
cleared the log fence and disappeared from sight, her
long strides carrying him out into the countryside. A
flash of lightning splashed its brilliance over the wide
field and thunder rumbled in the distance.

'We'd better head for the car.'

Angela grabbed a small, grubby wrist in each hand
and Madeleine turned to help her with the rug as the
rain poured down, soaking through her cream cotton
dress in seconds. In another minute the rain had turned
to hail that slashed out of the sky, stinging her skin and
almost blinding her. Jordan! she thought in panic. How
could anyone ride in this?

Miraculously, the sky cleared only seconds later and
as it did Madeleine heard the announcer's voice.

'We have a faller at the Coffin. Number fifty,
that's——'

Jordan! Not needing to hear the name, Madeleine
abandoned Angela and, breaking into a run, headed back
towards the finishing line, ploughing through the muddy
quagmire that had once been the field, her mind just a
haze of panic. Jordan!

Her breath coming in aching gasps, she stumbled the
final few yards to the Coffin, skidded to a halt and stared
in bewildered disbelief. Nothing. Not a sign of Jordan
and Diamond. Water from her soaking hair dripped into
her eyes and as she tossed it back a movement, a flash
of grey and white drew her attention to the finishing line

a short distance away. With a sobbing gasp of relief she
saw Jordan pull Diamond to a slithering halt and slide
quickly from the saddle.

'Jordan!'

The seconds it took to reach him seemed an age, but
at last she was there, her hands going out to him instinctively. Then she stopped, frozen into stillness by the look
in his eyes, the violence with which he repulsed her
gesture of concern. He scarcely spared her a glance, his
attention concentrated on Diamond as he dropped to his
knees in the mud, his lean, strong hands smoothing down
the mare's legs, checking for any sign of injury, his face
a mask of absorbed concern.

'Horses, not people, have his heart.' Struggling against
the pain of Jordan's rejection, Madeleine didn't want to
remember Peter's words but they echoed over and over
in her head, gaining a new significance with each rep-
etition. Dimly she heard soft footsteps on the grass
behind her.

'Bad luck, Jordy,' an all-too-familiar voice drawled.
'That fall's going to cost you valuable points.'

Peter. Only he could sneer in quite that way, injecting
such petty triumph into each word.

Jordan had straightened up, his eyes going past
Madeleine to where Peter stood behind her, and the
change in his face worried and frightened her. She turned
reluctantly, meeting Peter's beautiful, mocking eyes
before her gaze was caught and held by the slim figure
at his side, a shiver of apprehension running coldly down
her spine.

'Hello, Jordan,' Sukey said.

Both Madeleine and Angela had taken a change of
clothes to the trials, ready for the end of the competition

when they would be needed to help with the horses once more, and after her soaking in the storm Madeleine hurried to the horse-boxes where, behind closed doors, she stripped off the sodden cream dress and pulled on her old jeans and a faded denim shirt.

The sun had come out again by the time she had changed, and she was standing in its warmth, trying to restore some order to her tangled mane of hair, when she saw the small, dark girl making her way cautiously through the mud towards her, the sight making Madeleine's heart sink to somewhere beneath the soles of her feet. She had been surprised and relieved at the ease with which the meeting with Sukey had passed off, the ugly scene she had anticipated never materialising. The younger girl had taken the news of Jordan's 'engagement' with a calmness and lack of surprise that convinced Madeleine that Peter had already been busy filling her in on the details, but now, seeing Sukey's expression, Madeleine felt queasy with tension, a flutter of apprehension starting up in her stomach.

Clearly Sukey had been safely ensconced in the shelter of the Evensleighs' Range Rover during the worst of the storm. Every gleaming dark curl was neatly in place, careful make-up enhanced those big brown eyes and she looked sprucely pretty in a bright turquoise skirt and white lace blouse, a heavy, ornate brooch pinned at her throat.

'So you're Jordan's latest.' The clear voice held a note of scorn. 'I understand that you're engaged.'

'That's right.' Piqued by the obvious implication of doubt in Sukey's tone, Madeleine lifted her hand to display the ruby and diamond ring on her finger. Such a brazen gesture would normally have been totally alien to her, but her determination to convince Sukey, combined with a private, stabbing regret at the knowledge that what she was declaring to be true was in fact a pretence, produced a reaction she didn't recognise in herself.

Sukey's dark eyes flickered contemptuously over the glowing stones.

'Very nice,' she said insincerely. 'But it doesn't mean anything.'

'Of course it does!' Madeleine kept a grip on her feelings with an effort. 'It means Jordan—loves me.' Silently she cursed that tiny hesitation as Sukey pounced.

'Does it? You must be very gullible if you've swallowed whatever story he's been telling you. Jordan collects women—picks them up and drops them as it suits him. He makes promises, but he never keeps them.'

'He means this one!' The lie burned in Madeleine's throat.

'Don't you believe it.' A sneer distorted Sukey's pretty face. 'There's only ever been one woman who meant anything to Jordan, and that's me!' Sukey's voice sounded shrill in the quiet air. 'Jordan and I go back a long way. We've had our differences, but that's all behind us now. I'm prepared to forgive and forget, and when Jordan knows that——'

'How can you be so blind?' Madeleine's control snapped. 'Jordan has nothing to give you but friendship. If you're wise you'll accept that, because if you don't you'll destroy anything he does feel for you completely.'

Who was she really warning? Madeleine wondered miserably. Sukey or herself? Didn't her words apply to both of them?

'Friendship!' Sukey spat the word out, completely unaware of the tender spot she had touched in Madeleine. 'Don't give me that! Listen, lady—I'll tell you how much

Jordan cares for me,' the malevolent voice hissed in Madeleine's ear. 'He killed his bloody horse rather than hurt me—can you say the same?'

So Sukey had seen Jordan's reaction at the finishing line earlier—and, although she knew that the girl had twisted the facts to suit her own ends, Madeleine had to bite down hard on her lip to keep back the sound of pain that almost escaped her.

'Do you love him?' Sukey asked suddenly, taking her unawares, so that the answer was written on her face before she was in control enough to hide it. 'Oh God, *do* you! You poor fool—enjoy your engagement while it lasts, because I swear I'll break it—I'll break both of you!'

'Madeleine?'

It was Jordan's voice, suddenly and surprisingly near. Turning wide, startled eyes in the direction of the sound, Madeleine saw how he had come up unnoticed, leading Diamond, and was now tethering the horse to the side of the horse-box a few feet away. The keen silver eyes took in her expression at once and he frowned, his narrowed gaze going to Sukey's face.

'What's going on here?' he demanded.

'Your fiancée and I were just having a little talk.' Sukey's tone was insolent. Her brown eyes rested on Jordan with a possessive gleam that made Madeleine feel sick.

'I see.' Jordan's voice was calm. 'Did Madeleine tell you we're to be married very soon?'

'No!' The word was a cry of shock, and for a second Madeleine felt desperately sorry for the other girl.

'Yes,' Jordan said firmly. 'We'll be married just as soon as it can be arranged. That's right, isn't it, Madeleine?'

The smile he turned on her was everything it should be; warm, loving, every inch the devoted fiancé. Pain wrenched at Madeleine's heart at the knowledge that it was all a pretence, a show put on for Sukey's benefit.

'No!' Sukey's voice was high and shrill. 'You can't go through with the farce, Jordan—it isn't true, it——'

Something in Jordan's expression pulled her up sharp, her small face whitening perceptibly.

'You're not going to marry her, Jordan!' The words were just a malevolent whisper. 'If you do, I'll make sure that you regret it.' Sukey's eyes slid towards Diamond standing patiently nearby and her hands lifted in a wild gesture towards the horse. 'I'll ruin your precious horse! I've done it before and I'll do it again— you'd better believe me!'

'I believe you.' All colour had left Jordan's face, but his voice was quiet and calm. Dimly, Madeleine recognised his tone as the one he used to soothe a nervous horse. All emotion seemed to have died in him, only his eyes were alive, wary and alert to every move Sukey made. 'I believe you, Sukey—what do you want me to do?'

The smile that crossed Sukey's face was hateful. 'I want you to break off your engagement. That ring you gave her——' She flung a scathing glance at Madeleine as she stood transfixed, unable to say a word. 'Take it back! Tell her you're not going to marry her!'

'Sukey, that's just blackmail.' Jordan's voice hadn't altered in the slightest. 'If I do it because you forced me into it, it doesn't mean a thing.'

'Doesn't it?' Sukey sneered, her expression one of gloating triumph. 'Oh, Jordan, how little you understand her! The silly bitch loves you! It will make one hell of a difference—I promise you it will!'

For a moment Jordan's composure slipped. Something flashed across his face, tightening the muscles in his jaw, and in the same second Madeleine felt a searing stab of anguish as she recognised that Sukey had won. She knew of Madeleine's love for Jordan and had used it heartlessly because, knowing too of Jordan's love for his horses, she was well aware of the fact that if he put Diamond first, choosing her before what she believed was a genuine engagement, then she, Madeleine, would never feel the same about him again. She lowered her eyes, unable to look at Jordan's face, too afraid of what she would see there, and Peter's words pounded in her skull, making her head reel.

'Madeleine?' It was Jordan's voice, quiet and questioning, and it jerked her into action. She couldn't stop the pain, couldn't change anything, but at least she could make it easy for him. She could save him from having to ask. With fingers that shook uncontrollably she tugged the ring from her hand and turned to Jordan, holding it out to him silently.

He didn't move. His eyes locked with hers, doubt, question and hesitancy showing dark in their silver depths. Was there anything more? She couldn't tell. Tears blurred her vision, and as Jordan still did not move she pushed the ring at him almost violently.

'Take it!' Sukey's voice sounded harshly in the silence. 'Take it, damn you!'

Very, very slowly, the slight movement seeming to take an eternity, Jordan reached out and took the ring from Madeleine's outstretched palm. The tips of his fingers brushed her skin, the light touch burning as if they were red-hot, and she almost doubled up from the pain that tore her heart in half.

Through the haze of anguish in her mind she heard Sukey's high, exultant laugh, but she had eyes for no one but Jordan. Her gaze was fixed on his face and so she saw the sudden change, the tiny flicker of a glance—towards Sukey, not Diamond. Then, quite deliberately, he caught hold of Madeleine's hand, turning it slightly, and with a firm, decisive movement pushed the ring back on to her third finger.

'Jordan, no!'

'Jordan!'

Madeleine's protest clashed with Sukey's wild shriek, but Jordan didn't spare the other girl so much as a glance. Still holding her hand, he drew Madeleine gently towards him, lifted the hand with the ring on it to his lips and pressed a long, lingering kiss on it.

'Be my wife, Madeleine,' he said clearly and confidently. 'Please say you'll marry me—and make it for real this time, because I love you and I don't want to live without you.'

Behind her, Madeleine heard Sukey give a small, choking cry and there was a blur of movement as the younger girl turned and fled. And all that time Jordan hadn't looked to right or left, but held Madeleine's eyes locked with his, the question he had asked still burning deep in them.

'Madeleine,' he said softly. 'Was Sukey right? Do you love me?'

'Oh, yes.' It was a sigh of happiness. 'I love you and——'

'And?' Jordan prompted gently.

'And yes—*yes*, I'll marry you, if it's truly what you want.'

'What I want?' Jordan's eyes darkened until they were almost black. 'Do you doubt that, Madeleine?'

How could she doubt it? Hadn't he just given her conclusive proof of his love when he had defied Sukey's threats, turning to her in spite of the danger to Diamond?

'Let me tell you something.' Jordan's hand tightened around hers. 'When I accepted Peter's challenge I was afraid, afraid that I had lost my nerve, that I was finished because every time I tried to ride I saw Sukey running towards me as she did on the day of the accident—but you changed all that. Today it was as if the accident had never been, because after last night I didn't see Sukey any more, all I saw was your face, and I wanted to ride—to win—for you.'

A gentle hand slid under her chin to lift her head as he spoke, so that she could look nowhere but into his eyes, and what she saw there made her head spin. No barriers, no steel shutters, he was completely open to her, the love he felt burning clear and unshadowed in his eyes, and she knew that those shutters would never be closed against her again.

'I meant what I said.' Jordan's lips brushed her cheeks as he spoke, his breath warm on her skin. 'I love you, Madeleine. I think I've always loved you, from the first time we met, but I was too closed in on myself, too determined not to let anyone come close to me ever again, so I couldn't let it out.'

'And now?' Madeleine asked shakily.

'Now I'm not afraid of anything. I love you. In you I have all I want, all I need. I want you with me for the rest of my life. Believe me——'

'I do,' Madeleine put in, her smile reflecting the warmth of her happiness. 'I believe you, my love.'

Jordan's arm slid round her waist, drawing her close.

'Let's go home,' he whispered. 'I need to be alone with you.'

He hadn't even glanced at Diamond, still standing patiently beside the horse-box, but Madeleine looked towards the horse and knew that she could afford to share him with his other love. She laid a gently restraining hand on his arm.

'You have a competition to win for me,' she said softly.

Jordan's sigh was resigned, but his smile was one of pure delight.

'So I have,' he said. 'But after that . . .'

'After that——' Madeleine echoed, but her words were lost against his mouth as he gathered her up in his arms and kissed her with a passion that promised an eternity of happiness.

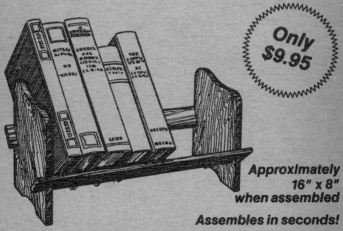

*Exciting, adventurous, sensual stories
of love long ago*

On Sale Now:

SATAN'S ANGEL by Kristin James

*Slater was the law in a land that was as wild and untamed
as he was himself, but all that changed when he met
Victoria Stafford. She had been raised to be a lady, but
that didn't mean she had no will of her own. Their search
for her kidnapped cousin brought them together, but they
were too much alike for the course of true love to run
smooth.*

PRIVATE TREATY by Kathleen Eagle

*When Jacob Black Hawk rescued schoolteacher
Carolina Hammond from a furious thunderstorm, he
swept her off her feet in every sense of the word, and she
knew that he was the only man who would ever make her
feel that way. But society had put barriers between them
that only the most powerful and overwhelming love could
overcome . . .*

Look for them wherever Harlequin books are sold.

Temptation™

TEMPTATION WILL BE
EVEN HARDER TO RESIST...

In September, Temptation is presenting a sophisticated new face to the world. A fresh look that truly brings Harlequin's most intimate romances into focus.

What's more, all-time favorite authors Barbara Delinsky, Rita Clay Estrada, Jayne Ann Krentz and Vicki Lewis Thompson will join forces to help us celebrate. The result? A very special quartet of Temptations...

- **Four striking covers**
- **Four stellar authors**
- **Four sensual love stories**
- **Four variations on one spellbinding theme**

All in one great month! Give in to Temptation in September.

Coming in April
Harlequin Category Romance Specials!

Look for six new and exciting titles from this mix of two genres.

4 Regencies—lighthearted romances set in England's Regency period (1811-1820)

2 Gothics—romance plus suspense, drama and adventure

Regencies

Daughters Four by Dixie Lee McKeone
She set out to matchmake for her sister, but reckoned without the Earl of Beresford's devilish sense of humor.

Contrary Lovers by Clarice Peters
A secret marriage contract bound her to the most interfering man she'd ever met!

Miss Dalrymple's Virtue by Margaret Westhaven
She needed a wealthy patron—and set out to buy one with the only thing she had of value....

The Parson's Pleasure by Patricia Wynn
Fate was cruel, showing her the ideal man, then making it impossible for her to have him....

Gothics

Shadow over Bright Star by Irene M. Pascoe
Did he want her shares to the silver mine, her love—or her life?

Secret at Orient Point by Patricia Werner
They seemed destined for tragedy despite the attraction between them....

CAT88A-1